Lucilla Andrews is a highly successful
and respected writer of fiction; and most
of her novels have a hospital setting. It is
a world she knows well, being herself a
State Registered Nurse who began her
career in 1939 and became a Nightingale
Nurse at St Thomas's Hospital, London
during World War II. She has been a
full-time writer since 1953, and lives in
London.

Also by Lucilla Andrews

IN AN EDINBURGH DRAWING ROOM
A WEEKEND IN THE GARDEN
THE PRINT PETTICOAT

and published by Corgi Books

After a Famous Victory

Lucilla Andrews

CORGI BOOKS

AFTER A FAMOUS VICTORY

A CORGI BOOK 0 552 12547 4

Originally published in Great Britain by William
Heinemann Ltd.

PRINTING HISTORY
William Heinemann edition published 1984
Corgi edition published 1985

This book is set in 10/11 Paladium

Corgi Books are published by Transworld Publishers Ltd.,
Century House, 61–63 Uxbridge Road, Ealing,
London W5 5SA, in Australia by Transworld Publishers
(Aust.) Pty. Ltd., 26 Harley Crescent, Condell Park,
NSW 2200, and in New Zealand by Transworld Publishers
(N.Z.) Ltd., Cnr. Moselle and Waipareira Avenues,
Henderson, Auckland.

Made and printed in Great Britain by
Cox & Wyman Ltd., Reading, Berks.

They say it was a shocking sight
After the field was won:
For many thousand bodies here
Lay rotting in the sun:
But things like that, you know, must be
After a famous victory.

Robert Southey

Part I

November, 1943.

1

Nurse Weston heard it first, that night. 'Convoy of sorts coming up behind, Kirby,' she warned, yawning and stretching her left leg to slow her brakeless bicycle against the nearside lane bank. It was her turn to save her headlamp's battery, so her machine was lightless and on the inside of the pair cycling abreast, but both nurses' night-acclimatised eyes could have managed without the single narrow pencil of light escaping the slit in the junior's blackpapered headlamp. No matter how dark the night, the countryside blackout was never as impenetrable as it could be in cities and towns and by that night in November 1943, petrol rationing had rendered almost non-existent civilian traffic on the mile of winding lane between the Night Nurses' Home and main entrance to Everly Place.

Everly Place was an Emergency Medical Services hospital that had replaced a peacetime mental hospital of the same name since early 1941. Nurses Weston and Kirby were the night staff of Male Orthopaedic 1 Ward, in the second month of their three-month term on night-duty. By now they knew every bend, bump and pothole in the narrow high-banked lane, and could – and when returning in the morning often did – ride it with one or both eyes closed. Occasionally on the returns one or other fell asleep, but as they invariably awoke when falling off their bicycles, they never hurt themselves or others. They never fell asleep riding to work; and even though neither was properly awake then, their ears were always on the alert.

That lane ran on beyond the Night Home and into

Avonly, a large village that was the nearest to the hospital; and the lane itself was a shortcut from one of the main roads running up from the English Channel coast and the main road to London that was just beyond the village. And at varying distances on the far side of Avonly were: since before the war, a RAF Flying Training School (F.T.S); since 1940, a Canadian Army camp; and since early this year, one of the many U.S. Army camps that had now become part of the scenery in rural southern England.

Nurse Kirby sighed sleepily and clamped on the brakes her husband had mended last week, when by happy chance her nights off had coincided with his unexpected leave. All the night nurses in Everly Place had three nights off after every twenty-one on. Sergeant Pilot Kirby, with his crew of C for Charlie, had been given five days' leave whilst their aircraft was refitted with a new port engine and various bits of fuselage after limping back to base from their last trip to Essen. C for Charlie was a Wellington bomber based in Oxfordshire, a county Michael and Susan Kirby regarded as being in the far north. They came from Eastbourne, and to them the north started at Watford. Everly Place was northish, as it was only about forty miles south of London. When they'd married last year, Michael had been 22 and Susan, 19. Sergeant Pilot Kirby was now in his second tour of operational duty and in the early hours of this morning had completed his forty-fourth night bombing raid on Germany. Susan Kirby was a smallish, sturdy, very pretty girl with soft, short, light brown hair that curled up around her long VAD cap and pushed it so far back that the small red cross at the centre front was only just visible.

The sound of the approaching engines was closer and she sighed again as, in practised unison, she and Nurse Weston leapt off and hauled their bicycles up the steep, wet, grassy left bank. 'RAF, Canucks or Yanks, they'll take every bend on two wheels. I'll bet the drivers are on a charge if they use four.'

'Probably,' agreed Nurse Weston vaguely, digging in

10

the heels of her flat, black, elastic-sided boys' house-shoes. She was of medium height and very slim and, having small hands and feet, she always bought boys' shoes for duty wear as they were comfortable, quiet, and had the even greater advantage of needing only two clothing coupons from the thirty-two that were the annual issue to adult civilians, instead of the five or seven demanded for 'womens' sizes. She balanced herself against her bicycle and wondered what odds 'Johnny' Player in Bed 18 would offer. Odds on. She smiled dreamily and resisted the temptation to share the joke. She thought Sue Kirby a sweet kid and not nearly as dumb as she looked or thought herself, but she had only been a VAD ten months; this was her first time on nights, and the only way to avoid all careless talk was to avoid careless talk. 'Whoever it is, is coming much slower than usual, Kirby. Night exercise, prob –' her voice stopped. The first of the oncoming vehicles had just crawled round the bend behind and the outline above the narrow shafts of light from the blackened headlights was unmistakable to both nurses.

'Ambulances!' Nurse Kirby was indignant. 'Who's gone round the bend, nurse? Night convoys never show up this early. Eleven to midnight's their E.T.A. [Estimated Time of Arrival]. This'll hit Cas, just on nine during the day and night staff changeover. It'll be –' her voice altered 'oh, baby. Rows of 'em.'

Nurse Weston stayed silent and both stood still and unseen in the darkness that on the banks was deepened by the overhanging pines and not yet wholly bare branches of the deciduous trees. The night was exceptionally mild for November; their outdoor uniform coats were bundled in their bicycle baskets with the small attaché cases holding their spare clean aprons and the three, lidded, Army mess tins containing their nights meals. Their navy cloaks hid the whiteness of their aprons and their caps and young faces only dappled with pale patches the darkly shadowed bank as the long convoy crawled on by. On and on.

'Salerno, nurse? You said this morning it was about time we started getting them back from there.'

11

'Only because of something Major Williams said when I washed him. I expect he'd had some advance gen on this from one of his visitors. His gen's always way ahead and right. Could be as he's Long Range Desert Group. The others say that bunch always knew what was happening in North Africa long before anyone else. Don't ask me how.'

Nurse Kirby didn't. 'Going on for ever.'

Rose Weston again fell silent. She was now wide awake though normally, at this stage on nights, that moment came when she walked through the main entrance of her ward and swung off her cloak. She was a trainee of St Martha's Hospital, London, an SRN for the last month, and in the second month of the fourth and final year of her general training. It was a heinous breach of Martha's etiquette for any nurse to wear her cloak one foot inside her ward or department and it had long become one of Nurse Weston's conditioned reflexes to switch on mentally immediately her hands unhooked her cloak collar.

The reflex functioned efficiently whether she worked in the much-bombed and still open Martha's, London, in Martha's Hut – the inter-hospital name for their main, county-evacuated branch – or in Garden East or Everly Place, the two vast EMS hospitals in this Sector that had Martha's nursing units amongst their multi-assorted staffs. The student nurses worked in rotation in these units spending between six and nine months in each and the remainder of their training in Martha's Hut or Martha's, London, but the last only once they were over 21.

St Martha's, London had first been badly damaged in the first London blitz that began in September, 1940. Long before the fifty-seven consecutive nights that event lasted were over, the Matron had introduced her rule forbidding minors to nurse in their parent hospital, to her additional relief when this suffered even greater damage in the second blitz that started in May, 1941. And as the war dragged on, it became a maxim in the scattered Nurses' Homes that the most essential attributes for any embryo-Martha were a suitcase large enough to take all her belongings but small enough to balance on handlebars, a bicycle, and the ability to ride it so loaded without falling off.

Nurse Weston was 25 and one of the oldest members of her set that was presently the senior on nights in Everly Place. Last April, when her set had moved here from Martha's Hut, the incoming convoys of newly repatriated wounded from North Africa had been fewer and shorter. Nearly all the men then arriving in England had been too severely wounded at El Alamein to withstand earlier the long voyage home on the hospital ships that since the end of 1940 had come and gone down the east coast of Africa, round the Cape, and up the Atlantic. Not all those ships ploughing through the torpedo-haunted waters reached their planned destinations, even although laden with men too wounded to fight again – as, with very rare exceptions, only those in this category were returned to UK hospitals. The others were treated in British services hospitals in Cairo, Alexandria, and other places nearer the sites of the campaigns. On discharge, patients were given sick leave locally and then sent back to their old or new units. In early May, the war in North Africa had ended and Everly Place had had a respite from incoming convoys just as, for all this year so far, London had been free from air-raids.

Nurse Weston's set had been grateful for the lull without expecting it to last. Wartime life, wartime news, wartime nursing had taught them to avoid such expectations, and taught them the fallacy of certain concepts instilled in them from early childhood – such as that the Great War that had killed so many of their own and their friends' fathers had been 'the war to end war', and that the great British Empire was undefeatable and permanent.

When her set entered Martha's Preliminary Training School in August, 1940, the Battle of Britain was being fought in the skies over southeast England. One month later, on the third night of the first blitz, their PTS Probationers' Home received a direct hit and in the small hours of a Tuesday morning they were all dug out alive and relatively unharmed after being buried for four hours in their Home's basement. Three weeks later another raid taught them that bombs, as lightning, often strike twice in the same place. When they emerged from their loaned dormitory basement of the Staff Nurses' Home, the mound of rubble that had been their PTS had become a massive crater. But their PTS term had continued to run its scheduled course in borrowed lecture and classrooms and on its completion they had been sent home for one week's holiday. Whilst at home, none had mentioned the bombing of the PTS to families or friends – a few because they were still too shocked to bear the recall; the majority, from their first insight into the simple truth that in any war, those not actively involved don't really want to hear about it, and those that have been involved either won't, or can't talk about it, until the raw edges have begun to heal. It took them all very much longer than one week to discover that the length of the healing time varied with the individual and could take from days to decades.

After that holiday they found themselves junior pros in the hastily evacuated main branch of Martha's, then in the process of converting into a general teaching hospital a conglomeration of Nissen and wooden huts on a country hillside recently evacuated by the British Army. Why that Army was then apparently being posted overseas whole-sale would have confused those pros more had their feet not hurt so much. Since the Fall of France in June, Great Britain and her distant Commonwealth had stood alone against the seemingly undefeatable German Army that now occupied the European coastline from the tip of Norway to the base of France. Occasionally, one pro wondered aloud what would happen if Jerry had another go at invading, and another replied that should be OK as the Canadians were defending England and Wales and the Poles, Scotland. Then the rest of the set insisted they stopped binding about the ruddy war and remembered Sister Tutor's saying yesterday that if all lectures weren't written up-to-date by tomorrow she'd report the dilatory to Matron. Then, as throughout their training, lectures

14

had to be attended during their daily three hours off, if on day duty, or between 9 and 10 a.m. after a night's work, on night duty, and all studying had to be done in their free time.

Their first-year examinations were looming, when 'Hey, girls, Jerry's gone up the wall and invaded Russia! So we've got a new Ally. Here's a turn-up for the books – talking of books – who's scrounged my *Notes On Nursing*?' That examination was safely over by December 1941 and they were junior second-years in the 2000-bed Garden East EMS hospital when the shock wave of the unannounced, unprovoked Japanese attack on the US Naval base at Pearl Harbour ripped around the world – and through the huge wards of Garden East filled mainly with RN and merchant seamen. The sick and wounded sailors smiled grimly, 'Oy, oy. Yanks'll have to jump off the fence.' And just a week later, before there was time to take in the relief of acquiring the most powerful of all Allies, those sailors' wards were stunned to an agonised silence by the news that the Japanese had sunk the battleship *Prince of Wales* and the battlecruiser *Repulse* on 10 December 1941.

Shock wave after shock wave. That Christmas, Hong Kong, taken by the Japanese; and in February, 1942, Singapore, taken. This last, the greatest Far East base of the British Empire, would have been unthinkable to those second-year student nurses born and raised when the map of the world was splashed pink by the Empire, had they not by then accepted the unthinkable as part of the natural order of wartime life. From their PTS onwards, someone's brother, boyfriend, fiancé – Missing; Missing believed killed; Killed in action. After Singapore in their set, four brothers, two boyfriends, one fiancé . . . Missing believed . . . Singapore became an unmentionable name inter-set just as once, long ago in the PTS, no one mentioned Dunkirk when Rosie Weston was around. 'No use talking, no use binding. Who wasn't browned-off with the ruddy war? And plain crackers to think one could take a breather because so many hospital exams and Preliminary

State were over. Big two still ahead. State Finals in October and toughest of all, Hospital Finals in January – say that again? We're shifting to Everly Place next week? Senior Sister Tutor's crackers! Everly Place is bursting at the seams and – hold it! Rommel, his Afrika Korps and the Italians have packed it in and we'll have time to flog the books – God bless General Montgomery and the Eighth Army and please, Monty or Alex or whoever don't invade anyone else just yet . . . oh, God, we're invading Sicily . . .'

The Allies invaded Sicily first on 10 July, and again some weeks later, the night convoys returned to Everly Place. The hospital had approximately 1400 beds and one of the most renowned orthopaedic units in southern England. From its opening in 1941, the Orthopaedic Unit had been filled and regularly enlarged to take civilian air-raid casualties from London and the continuously increasing numbers of wounded servicemen, as the predominant injuries resulting from skies raining steel, shrapnel, bullets and explosives were mangled bones, flesh and burns. To the profound secret relief of Nurse Weston, the Burns Unit for that Sector was in Garden East and when her set had worked there they had been too junior to be allowed into the BU for more than errands. She had a good memory and imagination; and the remembrance of those fleeting visits still made her shiver violently.

Before this move to nights in MO 1, she had worked as senior student nurse on days in Hut 9, one of the several long, 40-bed wooden hut wards in the Orthopaedic Unit, and mainly filled with Other Rank servicemen and a few male civilians. This August, whilst she worked there, new place names had begun displacing Tobruk, Benghazi, Mersa Matruh, Longstop Hill, Bir Hakim, Hellfire Pass and Alamein in ward conversations. Sicily, Syracuse, Augusta, Primosole Bridge . . .

'What was that, sergeant? Plimosorry?'

'No, no, Nurse Weston, Primosolly – that's right, nurse, paras took it – what you mean whose paras, Dusty? Do us a favour – read your flipping papers – if you'll pardon my French, nurse – Our paras took it. 'Course!'

This September; 'You hear what I just heard on the wireless, Nurse Weston? You hear, Dusty? Yeah – that's right, mate – pitched old Musso out the Eyeties have – come again, nurse? What's that? Co-belligerents? Us and the Eyeties? Getaway!' And the loudest and longest shout of laughter ever heard in Everly Place had deafened the long wooden ORs hut wards and the single-storey brick-built former mental up-patients' villa that was Male Orthopaedic 1, a 28-bed combined services officers' ward.

When the laughter faded, more grim smiles in Hut 9. 'Not all over bar the shouting yet it isn't, Nurse Weston. Not with old Jerry still on the job. Jerry's a fighting man, he is, and he don't give no ground easy and he'll not pack it in easy. Mind you, nurse, our lads'll show him the door Italy same as we showed him the door Africa and then it'll be next stop Berlin and all change for civvy street. Roll on the day?'

The long convoy had rolled on and, from the reverberating crashing of gears, had begun turning in through the wide gateless entrance some two hundred yards beyond the bend ahead. Nurse Weston slithered her bicycle back onto the lane and thought aloud, 'Messy show, Salerno, he said this morning. Messy.' Her wide, kind, unpainted mouth smiled without humour. 'Three days and three nights under non-stop bombardment on that beachhead. Chaps must've been quite glad to get off that beach, he said.' She scooted to mount and as she rode ahead in the darkness the large bow at the back of her small, starched muslin cap fluttered like a butterfly trapped in the thick coils of her high black bun.

Nurse Kirby, speeding to draw abreast, announced brightly, as always when disturbed by the war, 'Thank God we've got a Navy.'

They rode on in silence listening to the continuous crashing of gears of the convoy snaking uphill to the Casualty Department that lay to the left of the Main Block, about one-third of a mile from the main entrance. That Main Block had once been a Regency country mansion in a private estate, built at the highest point of the semi-clearing of a long, lowish wooded hill, to look down on sculptured parkland. The wood behind and above the house was still there and for most of the year alive with birdsong, the cries of rooks and rifle cracks of the wood-pigeons' flapping wings. The sculptured parkland had begun to disappear during the mental hospital's tenure when the old house had been renamed Administrative Centre and the brick villa wards built. The EMS had altered the name to Main Block, and added to its imme-diate left and right the large Nissen huts that housed respectively, Casualty and X-ray, and the Orthopaedic and Plaster theatres.

Inside the house, the Matron's, Medical Superintendent's and the one small office shared by all the consultants, and even smaller resident medical staff's common-room, that all occupied a part of the ground floor had been left intact. The rest of the ground floor and the whole first floor had been converted into a smallish, modern, and, by wartime standards, well-equipped General Surgical Unit. This consisted of a theatre and two 14-bed wards that were unique in Everly Place, as all the beds were proper, white-framed hospital beds on castors, and every bed had a proper hospital locker and, fitted to the wall behind it, a bedhead lamp and a plug for wireless headphones. All the other wards had individual wireless sets donated by the British Red Cross and St John's Ambulance Societies and the sets' users were usually restricted to the BBC Home Service news bulletins and, especially in the Orthopaedic Unit, the Light Programme in the evenings. All sets and headphones were switched off between 9 p.m. and 7 a.m.

The EMS had removed and replaced with cement the old lawn in front of the house to provide the ambulances yard, the merging point of the inter-hospital roads that stretched grey tentacles to all the new wooden hut and old brick villa wards. Huts and villas lay in a widely spaced descending horseshoe from Main Block, whose nearest ward neighbour was MO 1, roughly 100 yards down the inner road; and the furthest, Male Medical 4, a brick villa half a mile away. As MO 1 was the nearest ward to the hospital's main entrance, its successive night nurses were invariably the last to leave their Home when going on duty.

By day and night, Main Block was the heart of the hospital. It housed the inter-hospital tannoy – switched off 9 p.m. to 8 a.m. – the outside and inter-hospital telephone switchboards, and the Matron's Office that was the nocturnal base of the Night Sister and her two Assistant Sisters, and was the official, if seldom used, base of the medical staff.

The incessant demand for young doctors by the Armed Forces had reduced to near-skeletal proportions the resident staff in most British civilian hospitals, and the EMS came into this category. All of Everly Place's few housemen were within six months of qualifying and once over the six months, with very isolated exceptions, all the able-bodied were called up. Young, able-bodied registrars were even more scarce, as for each, their parent teaching hospitals had to request the special two-year deferment only granted those already Members of the Royal College of Physicians, or Fellows of the Royal College of Surgeons. Once the deferment period ended, the able-bodied vanished into the Forces whether or not the civilian post they had left vacant had been filled.

This situation presently obtained in the Orthopaedic Unit. A month before the last orthopaedic registrar had disappeared into the Navy; he had not yet been replaced and his work was being shared by the hospital's two consultant orthopaedic surgeons, Mr Hodges and Mr Arden. When the registrar left their only assistant had been their shared houseman, but early last week by pulling every official and unofficial string available, they had managed to acquire a second houseman. His name was Mr Lomax and he'd been qualified five weeks. 'If the law of the land allows the young ignoramus to sign a Death Certificate, who are we to quibble, Joe?' boomed Mr Hodges to his considerably younger colleague. Mr Hodges was a large man in the early fifties with the powerful shoulders, arms and voice that were not infrequently found in orthopaedic surgeons and being one of remarkable skill and long experience, habitually referred to himself as 'a mere bloody bone-setter.' Mr Arden shared Mr Hodges's height, shoulders, skill and professional attitudes, but was four stones lighter and not in the habit of using his deep voice as a megaphone or ever referring to himself. 'Apt, Bill,' he replied.

Mr Lomax was 23, small, fair and shy, and had qualified in an English provincial teaching hospital out of the range of enemy bombers. And as happened so often now the war had gone on so long, though the whole country shared the blackout, rationing, shortages, omnipresent uniforms, war anxieties and war news, those areas 'out of the war' tended to forget what was going on elsewhere even when elsewhere was in the next county. Mr Lomax's first impression of Everly Place on a sunny late October morning, was that it must contain half the British Army. Wherever he looked were young or youngish men wearing service or forage caps, in wheelchairs, wicker spinal carriages, on crutches, on sticks, and all with either one or more limbs in plaster, or missing. It took him a couple of minutes to register the numbers of women of all ages and older men in the same predicaments. 'All civvy air-raid casualties?' he demanded incredulously of Mr Thomas, the newly promoted Senior Orthopaedic Houseman.

'What else? Jerry sends the OU our civvy and service customers. The medical and general surgical sides get theirs from the usual channels – mostly from London – but Jerry's lent a hand there by flattening so many London hospitals. We poor sods in OU [Orthopaedic Unit] owe him every ache in our poor bloody feet and backs. Got a bike? My God, you'll need one. Not to worry. I know of one going for ten bob – dodgy brakes, no lamps and tyres've seen better days, but just the job. We'll – hold everything!' A very young blue-jacketed porter was waving like a tic-tac man from outside Casualty.

Mr Thomas bellowed, 'Who wants me, Bert?' and after more frenzied signals 'Thanks. Tell him I'm on my way.' He turned to Mr Lomax. 'Sorry, old boy. Cope with the bike later. J.J. calleth and when he calleth, jump to it, lad.'

Mr Lomax scampered after him. 'Who's J.J.?'

'Joseph John Arden.' Without pausing his stride Mr Thomas respectfully tugged his forelock. 'Old Bill Hodges is the one with the bark. J.J. leaves the scars. Show you mine, anon. You've got to meet him. Look lively, lad. Just close your eyes and think of England.'

'Scotland,' corrected Mr Lomax breathlessly but firmly.

'Mr Lomax is not wholly without promise,' pronounced Sister MO 1 seating herself at the small deal dutyroom table and opening the large ward log book. 'But he has much to learn.'

Nurse Weston upfolded the outer corners of her clean apron skirt with unusual deliberation before taking the opposite chair. 'Is Mr Lomax assisting admitting the convoy, Sister?'

Sister MO 1 inclined her impressively capped, neat, iron-grey head. She sat straight-backed and with every line of her old, beautiful face set in its customary, impassive sternness. 'Yes, nurse. For the first time.'

Nurse Weston looked up quickly and glimpsed the expression at the back of Sister's dramatically dark eyes. I've only worked in one world war, she thought, Sister's had two. France and Salonika, last time. But even Sister, nursing since 1912, was shaken rigid as the rest of us when we admitted the first ex-PWs from Italy. 'Do we yet know who's in this convoy, Sister?'

'From the little I could learn from Matron's Office when I took up my daily report at half-past eight, most of the wounded are from Salerno. I regret not being able to tell you how many we may expect. We have four empty beds and eight emergency beds in our storeroom. If you require more the night porters must bring them from the General Store.'

'Yes, Sister.' She folded her hands in her lap and thought,

if we need more that'll take ages with only two night porters to cover the whole hospital, so if we take more than twelve they'll have to have mattresses on the floor till their beds arrive. There won't be enough stretcher trolleys – there never are – soon as one arrives the patient has to be lifted off to free the trolley for the queue waiting to be lifted on – but as that's routine, stop binding, Rosie! She used her set's variation of her name unconsciously and from a habit that dated back to the PTS when she had shortened her given Christian name Rose-Anna as the combination of Rose and her married name had given her a new identity. And worked, she thought now. No one, not even her set, remembered, if they had ever known, her maiden name or had ever seemed to connect her with her late paternal grandfather. No one, apart from the Matron of Martha's who, in consequence had allowed her to jump the queue to enter the PTS. 'Sir Henry was, in his lifetime, one of our most valued Governors,' had said the Matron in Rose Weston's first interview. The Matron had not mentioned what else her grandfather had done in his lifetime and nor had his only grandchild to anyone since she started nursing. Nor, since then, had she ever been able to forget what had been the cornerstone of her grandfather's great wealth.

Sister MO 1 smoothed her starched cuffs as was her mannerism when about to begin a handing-over report. All these reports were given in the small, cramped dutyroom that stood just beyond the ward kitchen down the narrow passage running from the inner wall of the entrance hall that divided the senior and junior ends of the long ward. As the dutyroom was out of sight and hearing of the patients, the reports were attended only by senior nursing staff and whilst they were in progress, the juniors remained in, or within hearing of the ward. The dutyroom contained the villa's one telephone, whose bell was audible from the hall if all the doors between were open. It was a strict MO 1 rule that the hall passage door must never be closed, that during reports the dutyroom door could be left just ajar, and must only be shut when the room was in temporary use for consultations, waiting relatives, or when Sister was giving a serious reprimand or bad personal news to one of her nurses.

'No admissions today, Nurse Weston. No discharges. No transfers. 4 empty beds. 24 patients. 21 bed-patients. 3 up-patients. No patients on the Dangerously Ill List. 1 patient on the Seriously Ill List. Senior Officers' Ward, Small Ward 1, Major Williams, Seriously Ill List . . .'

Nurse Weston listened intently to the detailed report on Major Williams's swinging temperature and the pus still soaking the dressings over the window [aperture for drainage] cut in the upperside mid-calf of the hip spica plaster of paris that encased his right leg from waist to toes. And listening her downcast glance fell, at first unseeingly, on her wedding ring, and then with a slight shock of recognition. Sometimes, these days, she found herself wondering how that ring had got there. Dunkirk now seemed as pre-war as the phoney war that had preceded it. Back in the dark ages before we started winning battles – take a grip, Rosie! Listen! God only knows how many we'll get in, when the night rounds'll start, who'll do them and if the only man they can spare for us is little Lomax though he means well what he doesn't know about orthopods could fill the British Museum Library wherever that's been evacuated to if it has – lay off and listen! You're running the shop till eight tomorrow morning with only Kirby, a good kid, but untrained and worried stiff about her Michael though she does her damndest about keeping that to herself.

'Small Ward 2, the Brigadier . . .' the well-modulated, impeccably professional voice ran on from SW 2 to the first of the four beds on either side of the portion of the ward reserved for senior officers (majors and over) and known to all MO 1 including Sister unless giving or receiving reports, as the West End. The 18-bed junior officers' portion was the East End and at both far ends of what had once been a single long ward, were set side by side two red-padded cells fitted with single beds and plain deal open barrack-room type lockers and renamed Small

Wards. On paper these were reserved for general officers and when so used, evoked ecstasy in the East End. Ecstasy died fast when a Small Ward was occupied by any MO 1 patient on the DIL, and that event automatically welded West and East Ends into MO 1. MO 1 dreaded the appearance of a red DIL label on a bedticket – the file of notes topped by the temperature chart and dogclipped to the billboard that hung from the lower front footrail of every bed. MO 1 began to breathe out when the red label was replaced by the yellow of the SIL. Flap all but over, chaps. Just a question of time. As every ward, MO 1 was filled with individuals but in good or bad moments spoke with one voice.

Rose Weston had learnt to recognise every nuance in that voice and as the report progressed through the East End, a note in tonight's chorused 'Here come our night nurses! Evening, nurses!' troubled the back of her mind. It's the convoy, she thought, as she had before she had unhooked her cloak collar. Always hits 'em here as it hit them in Hut 9. They mayn't know any admissions we may get, but they know that with some they'll have, or have had in common, friends, mates, oppos, whose names they've missed in the casualty lists as either they were too ill to read or be told of the lists when they came out, or the missing names haven't yet been listed as more than 'Missing' as their owners' bodies haven't yet been found, or were found too mutilated for identification as the pieces with the dogtags were missing. But somewhere, some soldier'll know what's happened to his missing mate; after every battle, some soldier, somewhere, always knows. He'll have told someone in his unit or what's left of it, that someone'll have passed it on and no signaller in any Army gets news round faster than the private bush-telegraph of the men that actually do the fighting.

Every man in MO 1 tonight has done that, she thought, and not just in one battle. Battle after battle – till their wounds wrote them off as fighting men and sent them 'home' to MO 1. Not that they ever talk about this, or of their futures in civvy street with one, or more, limbs missing. They never say how they feel about the convoys. They just pretend to laugh and lay illicit sixpenny bets with 'Johnny' Player on how many we'll get in and how many on stretchers, how many walking-wounded. And 'Johnny' with both feet and two-thirds of his left leg missing will laugh like a drain if the bank cleans up and by this time tomorrow any newcomers not under anaesthetics, or morphia or in coma will have been sworn in to Johnny's book that no patient has ever mentioned to the staff and would have the Army on Johnny like a ton of bricks and Sister getting hell from Matron, if the word got out. It won't. Sister'd go to the stake before she'd deprive MO 1 of one of its best morale boosters, and my God is she right! They need it – especially on nights like this. That odd note in tonight's big hallo was as throttling as the ward atmosphere after the clean country night air. And that's always the same, too.

For the last several weeks, when the night nurses arrived at five minutes to nine, the early blackout of the shortening days, had thickened the ward atmosphere to a penetrating mixture of fresh and stale tobacco smoke, warm rubber undersheets, raw carbolic, ether, iodiform, anaesthetics, anthracite, starch, talcum powder, methylated and surgical spirits, the sickly-sweet aroma of drying new plaster, the sickly-acrid smell of drying and dried pus on old, sweaty plasters, and the boiled-over cocoa the up-patients in the self-enlisted kitchen crew began brewing themselves as one of their recognised pre-first-night-drinks-round perks at 8.25 when Sister or the day nurse in charge left to hand in the day report to Matron or her deputy, and Ellie, the ward maid had gone off duty. Ellie was officially off at eight, but as she regularly informed MO 1, she, for one, was no clock-watcher. She had been for twenty years Sister's ward maid in London and had volunteered to accompany Sister to Everly Place in the first Martha's unit in early 1941. On the day following their arrival, Sister, with Ellie, had opened MO 1. Ellie put this the other way round. And by that night in November, 1943, it was the long-held conviction of MO 1 that to take

25

on single-handed and weaponless a panzer division would be a piece of cake in comparison with taking on Ellie.

The kitchen added its own touches to the atmosphere; the mustiness of perpetual condensation; the reek of the cockroaches that neither regular fumigation nor pounds of anti-cockroach powder had been able to eradicate for more than twenty-four hours at the outside. When Nurse Kirby had first come on nights, she had been nearly as shy of the transient kitchen crew as terrified by the cockroaches, having been totally unaccustomed around any kitchen to the sight of the sort of young men she had met at the tennis club where she had first met Michael Kirby. Familiarity had bred in her a resigned horror of the cockroaches and a deep affection for her patients that had unconsciously filtered into letters to, and telephone conversations with, her husband.

Sergeant Pilot Kirby was a self-assured, competent, strong-minded young man – to the constant gratitude of his crew and more resigned gratitude of his Wing Commander who had been forced to accept young Kirby's adamant refusal of a commission. But as Michael Kirby was very much in love with his wife, he had decided on his last leave to do a spot of reconnaissance. He'd never been wounded, but had heard – who hadn't? – what officers' wards were like. He had known, but having a strong streak of self-preservation, never let himself dwell on the thought that wards like MO 1 existed in RAF and other service hospitals. Sister MO 1 had given permission for him to pay a short visit to her ward. Sergeant Pilot Kirby had returned from leave feeling relieved and acutely guilty in more senses than one. For other reasons his visit had relieved MO 1. From Nurse Kirby's first night, MO 1 had privately nicknamed her Sweet Sue and had her number: 'Married her first boyfriend with Mummy and Daddy's approval. Didn't suspect the facts of life existed until the honeymoon and still believes there are fairies at the bottom of the garden. Sitting duck for wolves if that lucky sod hadn't seen her first. He's all right – not a bad type, actually . . .'

26

Nurse Kirby, repressing a shudder swept a cockroach off the dresser to deposit on it her attaché case and the six lidded mess tins. 'Good evening, gentlemen and thanks awfully for starting my drinks round.'

Major Grover, R.A., the present crew's cook, smiled over his shoulder whilst stirring with a wooden spoon in his good right hand, the eight-pint cocoa saucepan. The stump at his left wrist was hidden by a sling; his left leg was in a below-knee walking plaster and his stick was propped against the electric cooker. He had been in MO 1 since June and sustained his present wounds in the third week in March during the successful British attack on the Mareth Line. In dressing gown and pyjamas he looked the youngish middle-aged schoolmaster he had been in peace-time. 'Good evening to you, nurse. Sleep well?'

'Gloriously, thanks.' Her very pretty face lit up at the memory of Michael's phone call after breakfast this morning. 'You all had a good day?'

The three-man kitchen crew smiled with pleasure for her and themselves. Sweet Sue was everyone's poppet and no one's popsie and just looking at her was a shot in the arm, especially when she smiled. And as her smile broadcast the question was safe, Captain Carteret, one-handedly setting large china mugs on the top shelf of the big wooden food-trolley, asked, 'What's the old man chalked up now?'

'Forty-four. Only sixteen to go.' Nurse Kirby swiftly set on a small papier maché tray a matching white cup and saucer, a combination that was the Brigadier's sole pre-rogative. 'Then grounded for another glorious three months.'

'Why didn't I join the RAF? Thanks, Bobbie.' Captain Carteret fielded the newly washed mug lobbed from the left draining-board by Lieutenant Dixon. Captain Carteret was Michael Kirby's age and had been in a Guards regiment before volunteering for a commando unit. His right arm had been blown off during the first landing on Sicily and his body badly lacerated. The lacerations had now healed and as he was naturally

27

left-handed and had two good legs and feet, he was regarded by MO 1 and himself as being good as new. He was the crew's layer and pusher of trolleys or anything else requiring a shove and presently the ward's most active patient.

Nurse Kirby searched the cutlery drawer. 'Who's swiped our three teaspoons? I must have one for the Brig. and all three were here when I went off this morning.'

'Panic over, nurse. Teaspoon, general officers for the use of, coming up.' Mr Dixon triumphantly fished one from the washing-up bowl. Mr Dixon of the 19th/23rd was 21 and had been in MO 1 since February and fought his last battle at El Alamein. He sat on the draining-board with the good foot of his good right leg propped against an open newspaper spread over the edge of the kitchen table, his crutches propped against the right draining-board, and his left pyjama leg empty from mid-thigh. Having uninjured arms and hands, he was washer-up. 'The Brig. wants cocoa tonight, nurse.'

'He does?' She studied the list on the back of an old temperature chart made by Carteret just before she came on duty 'Thought he'd gone off cocoa.'

'Typical of brass hats. Always changing their minds,' announced Mr Dixon. 'Oh – sorry, sir.'

'If you must apologise, boy,' said Major Grover mildly, 'apologise for being obtuse. This is not a case of the Brigadier's changing his mind, but merely of his giving due recognition to the fact that my cocoa is infinitely more palatable than my predecessor Colonel Danby's and fast approaching Nurse Kirby's superlative brew. I'm a bit short on sugar, nurse. Can we spare more?'

She opened the store cupboard. 'Oh, yes. Masses, tonight.' She dumped a stone jar on the table and opened the refrigerator. 'Masses of milk, eggs and – no – not butter – marge. Sister must be expecting lots of admissions.' She missed the men's quickly exchanged blank glances . . . 'Sister's a wizard scrounger. Give points to the RAF.'

'And the whole bloody British Army. Okay to shove forth the cold milks, nurse?'

The trolley was back for the cocoas and Mr Dixon had slid nimbly to his good foot and was on his crutches when Sister, escorted by Nurse Weston as etiquette ordained, paused in the open doorway. 'Goodnight again, gentlemen.'

'Goodnight, Sister,' the crew chorused and each man noticed that Snow White – their private nickname for Nurse Weston – wore the composed 'time for all good little dwarfs to be tucked up in bed' expression that invariably appeared on her creamy, wide-set brown-eyed oval face when a flap was about to take off. It was perhaps a couple of minutes later and just after they had heard her reclosing the hall blackout curtains concealing the hardboard-battened double glass doors of the villa's main entrance, that she streaked by to silence the suddenly ringing telephone, and kicked shut the dutyroom door behind her. She hadn't forgotten the rule, now, how very clearly anyone talking on the dutyroom telephone could be heard from the kitchen if both doors were open.

'Male Orthopaedic 1. Nurse Weston, speaking.'

'And a nice little packet we've got for you, nurse,' replied the senior night porter's laconic voice.

She stiffened inwardly. Stan, the senior night porter never flapped and had the inter-hospital reputation of being one of its finest diagnosticians. She pulled her pen from her bib pocket and flipped up her apron skirt to make notes on the up-turned hem. 'Ready, Stan.'

'Ten officers. Four stretcher-cases, but just the one SIL Paraplegic. All stretchers, Salerno. Six walking-wounded – if you calls it walking – ex PWs, Italy. Mr Lomax is still sorting the PWs's notes but an ambulance'll have the lot along to you, smartish and if young Mr Lomax gets his head down atween his knees, he'll do. Seems he's never heard of the Eyeties ice-and-cotton wool technique – if you cares to call it that. Has now. And the Night Sister says to tell you she's sorry she can't spare you help to put up the extra beds but seeing MO 1's quiet tonight reckons you'll manage.'

Her eyes had so darkened they looked black and too big for her face. 'We will, thanks, Stan. Thank Night Sister.'

'Trust me, nurse. Half a tick – bit of news. This lot got fetched back through the Med. and not the long way round. Comes of being on the winning side, seemly. Thought you'd like to know that's what we are.'

'Thanks very much, Stan.' She put down, closed her eyes and shivered uncontrollably.

Five seconds later she was in the kitchen doorway. 'Sorry, gentlemen, I've got to swipe Nurse Kirby. Can you again be angels and finish drinks for us?'

'Haloes at the ready, nurse!' the men chorused and when the nurses vanished looked at each other in a silence that was broken by Mr Dixon's, 'Action stations, sir! Cocoa's boiling!'

2

Mr Aden was reading notes at Sister's desk when Nurse
Weston emerged silently from the two red screens round
34, the nearest to the hall of the five emergency beds in a
longitudinal line down the middle of the East End. It was
1.30 and the only illuminated overhead light in what had
formerly been one vast, wide long ward, was directly
above the desk in the hall. The flex had been pulled down
to within a couple of feet of seated heads. The white china
shade was draped with a red linen cover that shed a crim-
son poll of light over the desk and tinged pink the hall
darkness and the shadowy outlines of the empty wheelchairs and spinal carriages against the outer wall on either
side of the main entrance, and the spare black oxygen and
carbon dioxide cylinders lining the inner wall on both
sides of the open doorway to the lighted passage. Once the
main ward lights were out an old, dark brown rexine,
fixed-footed screen was opened across the doorway. Four
more half-open brown screens were fixed permanently on
either side of the hall ends of the ward's divisions to give
the impression of individual entrances to West and East
End and to protect the nearest beds from draughts from
the passage, and, in daylight, the main entrance. No
draught came through the hardboard-battened double
doors during blackout hours owing to the length and
thickness of the black curtains just inside.
    She looked thoughtfully at the surgeon's lowered head.
In that lighting his short, slightly curly pale brown hair
looked grey, his strong facial bone structure more pronounced; and the lines at the outer corners of his rather

31

hooded eyes and running down his flat cheeks and those of his not insensitive but uncompromisingly determined mouth, seemed marks of age rather than temperament.

'I'm sorry to have kept you waiting, Mr Arden,' she apologised in the flattened murmur used by all experienced night staff since it carried far less than a whisper.

He glanced up, briefly. 'When you discover how to be in two places simultaneously, nurse, let me know. It's a technique I can use. In any event, I've nowhere near finished this bumf.'

Oh, God, she thought, he's in one of his Big Doctor moods. Why couldn't Old Bill act-registrar here tonight? He'd have understood, patted me on the shoulder, said, 'there, there', asked if we could squeeze him a cuppa and told me everything I need to know about everyone. Not J.J. In and out on the double on past showing, only not tonight with all little Lomax's notes to check. And then she thought, what the hell? What if he did see me committing one of the greatest of all nursing crimes when he looked over the screens just now? If he knows how I could've held that poor one-armed boy weeping in my arms without sitting on the side of the bed – he can tell me. And if he wants to report me to Night Sister and she to Matron – let 'em!

She looked primly down her short, straight nose and said primly, 'Then will you excuse me whilst I change my apron and ask my junior to take Mr Richards a hot drink?'

He picked up the amended ward diagnosis list and glanced at the entry that read: EB34. Lieutenant R.N. Richards. Age 24. RA. PW 1. Amp. L. arm, stump approx. 3 inches, flap unhealed. 'Go ahead, nurse. I'll watch them whilst you're outside.' He didn't look up until she had disappeared into the screened passage and then he gave the screens round 34 in the darkened East End a long, guarded look.

Rose had her apron off before she reached the dutyroom. She took a clean from her attaché case, bundled in the dirty, washed her hands in the dutyroom sink then shot back to the kitchen putting on the clean apron. 'Thanks for laying on the scrambled eggs, Kirby. Could you nip another cocoa to Mr Richards? once he's had it, get his screens down if I'm still tied up with J.J.'

Nurse Kirby was at the sink and didn't turn round. 'Okey-doke, nurse.'

Rose looked at her back, then towards the hall, then went into the kitchen. 'He's snapped out of it. It was just –' she hesitated 'just relief at getting back alive.'

'I know.' Sue Kirby unnecessarily tightened a tap. 'Two others nearly wept into their scrambled eggs. Just happy, they said.'

'They all say that. And mean it.'

'Happy?' Sue Kirby swung round, her face flushed and eyes red-rimmed. 'Shuffling and limping in like exhausted scare-crows in outsize uniforms all with one sleeve or trouser-leg empty? Happy? How can you say that?'

Rose's half-weary, half-impatient sigh was an outward expression of her inner longing to howl with despair. 'Be your age, Kirby. You should know by now – and I've told you often enough – the only prisoners that get exchanged are the crippled, the blinded, the dying of tubercle or anything else that makes it dead certain they'll never be able to draw another gun on Jerry. Anyone with a hope in hell of that, Jerry's hung onto. If tonight's lot –' she gestured towards the hall 'weren't as they are, they wouldn't be with us now. They, like those they've left behind, would either be on their way to, or already in prison camps in Germany.' Seeing she was getting through, she went on quietly, and ruthlessly. 'Don't kid yourself every PW of Jerry's going to get back alive. Some will. Some won't. This lot, have! So tonight they ARE happy and some of them weep because they're too physically weak to control the tears. Why shouldn't they be happy? They've survived near-starvation and – God knows what else.' She paused a moment. 'All tonight's but Richards are married. Think of their wives tonight. Their kids. Think of Mrs Flynn – Captain Flynn's in 30 – he's 26 and he hasn't yet seen his 2-year-old son. All but Major Fraser's wife should be here tomorrow as she's got to come down from Caithness, but he told me tonight that when he managed to get a trunk call through after the ship docked she hadn't even known he was on his way back. Back. Safe. Home soon.'

'Yes, yes. I must – oh, baby –' Sue Kirby was half-choked by a new distress 'nurse, I'm terribly sorry I forgot your – I keep forgetting –'

'Skip it. Back in the dark ages. All right?'

'Yes, only – what's paraplegic?'

Rose had backed to the doorway. She looked quickly over her shoulder at the screened doorway then back at her junior. 'Tell you properly, later. Briefly, Captain Eccles got a bit of shrapnel thereabouts.' She half-turned her back and with one flattened hand tapped her spinal column just above the waist. 'No feeling, no control from there downwards.'

Sue Kirby went pale. 'Both sides?' Rose nodded numbly. 'For – for always?'

'Yes. 28.' She looked at the floor. 'I must get back. Get weaving with that cocoa.' She turned away and walked slowly enough back to the hall to have recovered outward control before she silently took the right-hand desk chair and discovered she was unexpectedly grateful Old Bill Hodges wasn't in the left. He would have greeted her return with one of his kindly, trite placebos about worse things happening at sea and at least this show hadn't yet turned up a Passchendaele or churned chaps by the million into the mud like the last show. Though to be fair, she recalled, he didn't often talk the Great War and when he did called it 'my war' and this 'your war' as he had spent '14 to 18' in the RAMC. Sister seldom mentioned it and J.J. never. J.J. only talked immediate 'shop' and only when he had to and when he didn't he kept silent. As now, after acknowledging her return by a faint lift of his eyebrows.

She was thankful for his silence and this first chance to sit down properly since the handing-over report, but the weariness of her back and feet were trivial against the weariness of her spirit. It seemed to her, just then, that she had spent this war drying the tears of others and concealing her own until she was alone and then she was either too drained of emotion, or too tired, or both, to shed them.

The desk at which they sat side by side, was an old card table covered with a dark blue cloth; their hard chairs had their backs to the screened passage and the shadowy cylinders lined up like headless sentries. From the lighted desk the darkness across the hall seemed deeper, the shadowy wheelchairs and spinal carriages strangely toylike, and the hall curtains and half-open rexine screens, great black smudges.

The pink tinge in the darkness of the divided ward was now much stronger in the East End. There were small, lighted, red linen shaded table lamps with long flexes on the floor at the hall side of 11 and 24, the two East End beds nearest the hall that had been empty when the night nurses came on and were now occupied by two of the admissions on stretchers. Captain Eccles was in SW3, which, like SW1, had a lighted lamp on the floor; and the combination of red shades and red-padded walls converted both into red caverns glowing into the darkness beyond their open doors. There was no light by 29, the only emergency bed up in the West End as the stretcher-patient it now contained was, by MO 1 standards, only moderately injured and should be out of plaster and off to Roehampton for his tin foot in a month or two; and there was enough light coming through Major Williams's door for the newcomer to see where he was and the nurses to watch him without using their torches.

Major Fraser, the senior of the ex PWs was in SW4. He had politely refused Rose's offer of a night-light. 'Not with the door open and the chaps just outside, thanks, nurse – er – forgive me, nurse, would you mind repeating that?' He was in the early forties, one-armed, thin as paper and looked an old man. Her repetition illuminated with wonder his grey, emaciated face. 'Scrambled eggs? Toast? Cocoa? For all us chaps – at this hour? Are you sure you can spare the food, nurse? Are you sure it won't be too much trouble, nurse? Oh – I say – oh, my word – yes, please, nurse! Thank you so much, nurse – thank you so much!'

Six times tonight, she thought at the desk. Almost identical words. Honestly, nurse? Sure you can spare – not too

35

much trouble – oh, God, yes, please – and – and thank you very much, nurse, thank you very much . . .

And, later, 'My God, I don't know what came over me, nurse – I'm most frightfully sorry – just that they were such bloody wizard scrambled eggs – but I'm frightfully sorry – God knows what you think me –'

'A very tired man, Mr Richards, who'll be flat out after another cup of cocoa.'

'Another? Sure you can spare – I say, thanks most awfully, nurse . . .'

We could've offered them the Holy Grail, she thought, turning her gaze from side to side, watching the sleepers, watching Nurse Kirby disappearing behind the red screens carrying a mug of cocoa on the small round papier maché tray, listening to the near-inaudible murmurs filtering through the cotton walls of the screens and merging with the snores, grunts, mutters, deeply-rhythmical respirations, the creaking of bedsprings, the gentle groaning of fracture boards under mattresses, the occasional chinking of the lead shot in metal buckets shaped like smallish shell cases that weighted the traction splints, as those patients on traction able to turn themselves turned in sleep that throughout MO 1 for some was natural and for others, drug-induced.

'Lomax writes here that Eccles had an extensive bedsore over his coccyx. Nothing about it in the notes that came in with him and I've just re-checked in case I missed it in Cas. There wasn't time there to get all his padding off. You found it, Nurse – er – ?'

'Weston, Mr Arden. Yes. Very extensive.'

He faced her for the first time since she'd sat down. 'Can you be more specific, please.'

'Yes, Mr Arden.' She held up her linked hands. 'I measured the depth of the ulcer with my hands like this and they fitted in to above my wrists without touching him. I take sixes in theatre gloves.'

'Don't move.' He framed her hands with his own without touching her. 'Good God,' he breathed.

She nodded and they dropped their hands and exchanged

36

a look that both had exchanged with other colleagues on innumerable comparable occasions but never before with each other.

'Does he know it's there, nurse?'

'He knows something's there. He said he thought it must be a bit of a bedsore as the sisters, particularly on the ship, changed his back dressings and turned him as often as they could and struck him as a bit upset when they couldn't get to him as often as they wanted.'

'Understandably. On all counts, hospital ships being no more overstaffed than this ward at night.' He glanced down at the old notes. 'From these, he was a bit chesty when first aboard, and a course of sulphonamides started stat. [medical abbreviation of the Latin 'statim'; English, 'at once'] cleared it up. Possibly it dealt simultaneously with the bugs cooking in the back ulcer, but only possibly, as the sulphas' range is limited. Where they can work, they do a good job, but there's the devil of a lot they can't touch.'

'There is.' She inhaled thoughtfully and detected the smell of pus in the heavy air almost with relief as the ugly, unmistakable reek of gangrene was missing.

He glanced at her more keenly as if seeing in her face something he hadn't expected to find. 'Lomax see the ulcer?

'No, Mr Arden. I'd re-dressed it and given Captain Eccles the sedatives you'd written-up in Cas. and he was asleep by the time Mr Lomax did his round. Captain Eccles was exhausted by the journey here, taking down the dressing would've woken him, so I asked Mr Lomax if it could wait till morning and he agreed. I hope you don't object?'

'No. How've you dressed it?'

'I packed the ulcer with tulle gras. [Medicated vaseline gauze.] It took a whole new tin. I've covered that with a thick dry dressing, wads of cotton wool and an abdominal many-tailed bandage. We've propped him on his right and I've put him on the two-hourly turns list. Luckily, turning from side to side doesn't seem to wake him any more than it does our hip spicas and spinals.'

'Experienced turners seldom wake 'em.' He glanced

from her slight shoulders and slender arms to the very pretty little VAD silently lifting away folded together the two red cotton-sided, fixed footed screens from 34. 'Eccles got any other bedsores?'

'No. The skin's in good condition over his hips, ankles, heels, elbows and shoulder-blades. He told me he's always healed well.'

'So he said in Cas. Nice chap.' His face tightened. 'Knows the score. Tell you?'

She looked down at the desk. 'Yes. He said he wanted to get it into the open and then not talk about it again. MO 1 knew before lights out. Long before. We didn't tell them. No one ever has to. They just get all the gen –' she snapped her left fingers quietly and her wedding ring glinted 'like that.'

'Patients do. Invariably.' He reached for the diagnosis list and tapped Lieutenant Richards's entry with the heel of his fountain pen. 'What specifically caused the crack? Homecoming?' He looked up as she didn't answer and read it in her suddenly widened, and darkened eyes. 'Plus re-admission?'

'Both, but mostly the second.' She spoke slowly and with a composure that made him study her with heightened interest. 'He didn't mention it, but I know he's terrified of the op. he must have to trim his stump before he can be fitted with a tin bit.' A 'tin bit' was OU jargon for any type of artificial limb. 'He knows – they all know – that's why they've come straight to us. None mentioned it, tonight. They never do on their first night and usually by the next day – well –'

'By the next day some of the raw edges are shifted by MO 1's habit of openly speculating on who's next for the chop and –' he looked deliberately towards 18, the furthest bed on the right side of the East End 'and so on and so forth. Right?'

'Yes, Mr Arden,' she said primly as they exchanged a conspiratorial glance that would have amused them equally but for what had gone before and must come.

'It's a rare patient who's not scared by the prospect of

any op., but when that natural apprehension's loaded by the memory of having an arm or leg hacked off, and bullets and shrapnel hoicked out without anaesthetics or morphia, with nothing but ice to freeze what could be frozen, straps and manpower to hold you down and a roll of cotton wool jammed between your teeth to stifle your screams and stop you biting off your tongue in agony, enough –' he continued in a tone that could have been discussing the weather 'to have the Archangel Gabriel in bloody hysterics. He didn't look hysterical to me. Was he?'

'No. Just tears.' She shuddered. 'Sorry. I know I shouldn't –'

'You'd be a-human if you didn't, nurse.' He stared into the East End and she saw a muscle twitching in his right cheek and the tightened right corner of his mouth. 'It's too bloody easy and bloody unfair to hand this can solely to the Italians. When their prison camp hospitals ran out of all medical supplies, Jerry should – and could – have helped them out. From all accounts Jerry's got ample medical supplies, they were fighting on the same side and supposedly, partners. Once the Italians had run out, what could their surgeons do but use what they had and what – bloody all they had – was ice, cotton wool and manpower.' He looked at her. 'Whilst not pretending there's no such animal as a sadistic surgeon, in my experience, the sadists don't often crop up amongst those that are really good at the job. Some of those Italian MOs must've been first-class surgeons –' he nodded towards the East and then West End 'there's the evidence. Three down the middle and Timson up in 3, all, at one time, developed gangrene in prison hospitals. Now, here. To get them here without anaesthetics, drugs, or proper nursing, some chap knew his job bloody well and did it bloody well.'

'Yes. I've thought that,' she said and felt near-lightheaded in her relief at being able to share this nightmare openly with someone capable of carrying his own share and not, metaphorically weeping on her shoulder as Mr Lomax had done, earlier. She had intentionally kept the whole truth from Sue Kirby, partially as the latter was so young for her age, professionally untrained, and so worried for her husband, and partially as it would have reduced Sue to a deluge of tears that she, Rose, would have tried to comfort, but probably unsuccessfully as Mr Richards's breakdown had left her so drained.

Mr Arden had returned to studying the diagnosis list in silence. But she sensed in his silence a new companionship and that it afforded them both that measure of consolation that often accompanies the discovery by comparative strangers that on certain basic issues their minds are in total accord.

She watched his lowered profile with a new-found curiosity. She knew little about him. No Martha's men worked in Everly Place. The majority of its medical staff, as Messrs Hodges and Arden, were from St Benedict's, London, a voluntary hospital on the opposite bank of the Thames to Martha's and the Benedict's nursing unit was the largest in Everly Place and, like the Martha's, had its own wards. There was little inter-unit communication between the two since both observed the voluntary hospitals traditional custom of keeping themselves to themselves. Had Joe Arden been a Martha's pundit, Rose, by her fourth year would have known for years the inside story of his private life and, roughly, what he had had for breakfast this morning. But her present ignorance was further accentuated by neither of the OU housemen being Benedict's men and privy from their student days to inter-hospital gossip on their new bosses.

All she really knew of Mr Arden was that he was a good, safe, surgeon – the two qualities didn't always go together – that the patients liked him even although, in her set's opinion, there was warmer blood in the Blood Bank fridges than in his veins, and that would have been enough to guarantee his remaining a widower since his wife died of pneumonia or something sometime before the war, without the obvious fact that at his age he was purely sisters' territory and one had only to look at the sisters in Everly Place to understand why any man should prefer to

40

stay single and rent a flat in the Hodges' house down the lane. Aside from the sisters there were no single women in what Rose and her set regarded as the right age for him in Everly Place; like everyone on the staff, he'd no time to meet any outside, and he was far too keen on his job and patently had too much nous to risk wrecking his career by making a pass at a married woman.

The circulation of these views in the Night Home had gained a new impetus in the last month when the two pundits had broken with long-established tradition by doing, generally on alternate nights, the night rounds of their non-existent registrar that brought them into direct contact with the OU night seniors. In consequence, Mr Hodges' great popularity had been enhanced, and if, in the main, Mr Arden's remained at its previous low ebb, it was agreed that he never wasted anyone's time and one knew where one was with him as if he didn't like something, he said so and anyone that thought his Big Doctor moods exceptional should try working with some of those Right Little God Almighties in Martha's. And anyway he was a Benedict's man and one had to remember there was a war on . . .

Not shooting his Big Doctor line now, thought Rose. He battens it under, but he really cares about the patients as much as Old Bill and he cares like hell. I should've worked this out from the way the patients like J.J. Pundits can sometimes fool their juniors into thinking them God's gift to suffering humanity, but they can't fool their own patients. No one can do that.

Mr Arden murmured to himself, 'Six must go somewhere in the morning and if they're to get to their new beds in daylight, go early. Theatre list starts at nine –' he glanced at his watch 'have to get busy on the 'phone by eight. Which six? Should be "ups" first, but Grover and Carteret still need hospital and not convalescent beds. Garden East can't take 'em and Roehampton can't take Dixon for another week.' He frowned at the list. 'We could send him home for a week's leave as –'

'Oh, no! Please.' The interruption was out before she could stop it. 'Sorry.'

41

He looked at her curiously. 'Tell me why you said that.'

She didn't hesitate now as this mattered too much to her; and he saw that. 'He's dreading going home till he gets his tin bit. His amputation has shaken his parents rigid, though they've tried to hide it when visiting him. But he knows it and that they're dreading what seeing his empty trouser leg'll do to his little brother and sister and that's worrying him stiff, too.'

'He's told you all this?'

She met his eyes. 'Yes, Mr Arden.'

He nodded to himself. Yes. It was always at night that the truth came out, but even on the darkest night that was only confided to a listener of proven sympathy and trust. He was unsurprised that the patients should trust this slight, black-haired girl bristling with starchy efficiency, but up to tonight she had seemed to him singularly lacking in the warmth without which sympathy was no more than lip service. He had been more than a little surprised when – who was it in the East End? Yes, Johnny Player – inadvertently let out her MO 1 nickname. He hadn't thought she possessed enough character, charm, maternal and sex appeal to fit the bill. Her pale, smooth, blank young face and wideset eyes thickly fringed with shortish dark lashes that, to his eyes, gave her an expression of prim gravity, had repeatedly reminded him of a wooden Dutch doll that belonged to one of his sisters in his childhood and had been left out in the rain one night and found in the morning with the red patches on the cheeks and lips washed away. It was only tonight, when he glanced over the top of Richards's screens and watched unseen for the few seconds before she glanced up, that the compassion in her downcast face, encircling arms and hand gently stroking Richards's head, and the small cap looking like a bow on her shining black head, had made her nickname immediately understandable. Then she had seen him, he had nodded to tell her to stay where she was and moved away thinking, apt. Bloody apt.

'Which six would you pick, nurse?'

It was the first time he had asked her professional

advice, but she didn't realise this, yet. She looked over both ends before turning to him with the unselfconscious assurance of an expert about to pronounce on her own subject. As he noticed. 'Certainly, Majors Aston and Small. They're getting browned-off and could use a change.'

He said almost apologetically, 'They've been stuck in hip spicas since they got back from Alamein, or have you some additional reason for the browning-off?'

'Yes. MO 1-itis.'

He guessed what she meant but wanted proof. 'How do you define that condition?'

'As one that hits those patients that feel they've had up to the back teeth the kind of prep school fun and games that goes on most of the time between flaps. Doesn't hit many but those it does it hits hard.'

'Who are most susceptible?'

'The civvy soldiers. I imagine this is because the Regulars must like being jolly chaps together and horseplay in the mess on Saturday nights to have chosen soldiering as a career.'

'I'll buy that one. All civvies?'

'No. Depends on their ages and brains. The brainy types of all ages have their own immunity as they like reading, playing chess, writing letters to their wives, girlfriends and so on, but particularly reading all the books they've never had time to read before. They take the fun and games like adults at a kids' party. Join in when they feel like it and opt out when they don't. It's the non-brainy civvies in the late twenties and early thirties that get MO 1-itis, as they're too old and too young for the party. The really old civvies in the forties like Major Grover' – she continued thoughtfully without seeing the flicker of self-derisive amusement in Joe Arden's grey eyes – 'take it all like indulgent fathers. So does the Brigadier, though he's the exception to my rule as he's a Regular and brainy, plus. I've always thought that whilst he's genuinely "dashed pleased to hear the chaps in such good form, nurse" he often thanks heaven fasting his red tabs and traction keep him anchored in SW2, but would face a firing squad before he'd admit it.' She looked back into the East End. 'Obviously, they all get browned-off, but when that happens most just shoot an extra line to pretend they aren't. Some are such good line-shooters –' her gaze rested on Lieutenant Player's bed 'that the line almost kids themselves. They get, but chuck off MO 1-itis. Some just can't. Not their fault. They just haven't sufficient natural resilience.'

To test her, he suggested drily, 'You mean guts?'

She raised her chin. 'No, Mr Arden, I do not. Guts and' – she gestured to both ends – 'MO 1 are synonomous terms. I know. I nurse MO 1.'

'Save that adrenalin, nurse. Point taken and accepted. Right. Aston and Small. And –?'

'Major Donkin.'

'MO 1-itis?' She nodded and he scribbled the three names on the back of an old envelope. 'Who else?'

'If you could get beds in a sector north of London it would suit Major Grover, as his home's in York, and Captain Carteret. His parents live near Leicester. Much easier for their visitors.'

'Might be possible. Worth the try. Last chap?'

She thought a moment. 'Mr Peters.'

'Why? He's got no family and I wouldn't have said he had MO 1-itis.'   •

'He hasn't, but he has got a WAAF girlfriend stationed in Oxfordshire near enough to Nurse Kirby's husband for him to give her a lift on his pillion when he came down for his last leave. Please don't ask me how he got the petrol for his motor-bike. I honestly don't know.'

'No business of mine how he got it. Right. Peters.' He added the name to his list. 'Who's Nurse Kirby? A Martha?'

'My night junior.'

His noncommittal nod wholly suppressed his surprise that that very pretty child should also be old enough to be married. He couldn't suppress his sudden acute awareness of being 42 and of the slight limp that had kept him out of uniform in this war and dated from the last month of the war that had ended before, as he assumed, either girl had been born. Knowing the minimum age for fulltime VADs was 18 and for entry to Martha's, 19, he put Sue Kirby at that last figure and Rose Weston around 22. 'Kirby, RAF?'

'Yes. On Wellingtons.' She smiled slightly. 'A Sergeant Pilot that won't be commissioned and coming from Sussex, won't be drove.'

He was amused by her rider and reluctantly fascinated by the changing expressions on her face that he had thought unexpressive. 'New one on me. You from Sussex?' She nodded and he found her silence so interesting that he returned abruptly to the matter in hand. 'I'll discuss these six with Mr Hodges and let Sister MO 1 know the score by eight-thirty. Don't say anything to the chaps until we're sure we've got them beds.'

'No, Mr Arden.' She listed the names on one of the strips of the backs of old charts dogclipped together for use as memo paper. The war had made paper so scarce that every available piece was hoarded for reuse.

She replaced her pen in her bib pocket and for a minute or two more they sat in silence, turning their heads from side to side and recognising the present – Rose from the recent and Arden from the more distant past – as a time that often occurred in wards late at night when the whole ward was sleeping well enough for the kind of conversation they had just had to take place and the combination of shared professional anxieties, fatigue, and the advent of the small hours lowered the defences enough to brush aside etiquette; and the mutual recognition of the affinity of their reactions to the realities of the moment temporarily transformed semi-stranger colleagues into close friends. Great fatigue alone levelled as successfully as sex, and both were very tired and grateful to be off their feet for a little longer, for the unstrained quality of their silence, and for the reassurance of the sleeping chorus flowing and ebbing from both ends like the waves of a quiet sea.

A new sound interwove with the waves. It was the sound of a distant aircraft with a limping engine, but neither remarked upon it nor glanced upwards. From the outbreak of the war no German bomb had fallen, or even been rumoured to have done, anywhere near Everly Place. But all this year, from time to time between 1.0 and 4.0 in the morning the hospital heard the hum of a bomber returning off course from one of the night raids on German cities made regularly by the RAF whilst the USAAF raided by day. Almost invariably the off course bomber's R/T (radio-telegraphy) and W/T (wireless-telegraphy) had been shot up and it was searching for the airstrip of the RAF FTS to make an emergency landing. All those heard from Everly Place in this year had landed safely.

In the kitchen, Nurse Kirby stopped cutting the bread for the patients' breakfasts to look upwards. She listened, intently. A Lanc, not a Wimpy, she decided and it couldn't be Michael, thank God, as he wasn't flying tonight and anyway the FTS was too far south for C for Charlie unless Michael, his navigator, and his compass had all gone haywire. But the nearest Lancasters' station was 95 miles northeast and she'd heard two or three lost Lancs before and occasionally a lost Halifax.

She usually knew when Michael was flying as when his station was operational it was closed for the twenty-four hours before each op. and he couldn't ring her. On the nights that she was sure he was flying, she dreaded the hours between 10.30 and 3.0 and every ring of the duty-room telephone from around 5.0 onwards seemed to stop her heart. 'In my business no news is good news,' said Michael, as if his business was a milk round. Last week his station had been rested; operational this week, so he wouldn't be able to ring when she got off this morning and tomorrow – no, it was now tonight, he'd be flying. Often three ops. a week when operational and when his station wasn't, others were. Night after night on the wireless news . . . Some of our aircraft are missing . . . NO! Mustn't think of that. She'd promised Michael and he'd promised her – if – please God, please – no – but – IF – his great friend on the station, a presently grounded Flight Sergeant would ring her on duty in the early morning and even

Night Sister would have to let that call through as that was one of Matron's rules.

'Not much longer,' Michael said on his last leave. 'Should finish this tour before Christmas. If so and they don't dish you Christmas leave, either I kidnap you or you go AWOL.'

Christmas. Only next month but years away. Sixteen more to go. Sixteen more times of flying into that ghastly flak and over enemy territory once he's crossed the Channel – all the way there – all the way back – forty-four times already. Sixteen more – no, I mustn't! That Lanc's gone and I must finish the wretched bread-and-marging and get today's emptied dressing drums filled whilst this quiet lasts. J.J. can't have gone as Weston hasn't put her head round to say all clear or had time to start writing Night Sister's 2 a.m. report and the old battleaxe'll go up the wall if it's not ready for her second round – but she'll be late as she was so late for her first and she starts with MO 1 – so we may have time to turn the plasters and that poor, poor bod in SW3 – what if it happened to Michael? No! I mustn't, I just mustn't – what was I thinking? Yes. If we can get them all turned I should get my meal before 3.0 and then take over the ward whilst Weston has hers with enough time in hand to make us a quick cuppa before we start work at 4.0. Oh, get off you repulsive monster!

She brushed a cockroach off the kitchen table and watching it scuttle to safety, thought aloud, 'Thank God we've got a Navy.'

3

'There goes my bloody jugular,' muttered Lieutenant Player of the West Saxon Yeomanry and, for the past week, Bed 19. He pitched his safety razor into the small bowl of hot water on the bedtable across his bed and grabbed the table to steady it as, with his bed, it was catapulted into the middle of the East End and Lieutenant Duncan.

'Mr Duncan, if you're doing what I think you're doing, please stop it, at once!' Rose called from behind the screens around 20 that was still backed against the outer wall. 'If you won't think of your new plaster, think of my neck when I have to tell Sister and the pundits you cracked it shoving out beds on your own.'

Mr Duncan mumbled incoherently and blushed pleasurably. He had an expansive heart and since his admission in February had rejoiced MO 1 by falling for a different nurse every month. October had been Snow White's; this one was Sweet Sue's; but December started next week and Johnny Player was offering 6–4 on the new day VAD known inter-MO 1 as Rita MacHayworth in her first hour on duty. Despite this, as Mr Duncan's amiable nature forbade his wholly casting off the old when taking on the new, he continued to enjoy looking at, reflecting upon and blushing over Nurse Weston's slender white neck.

'Don't flap over Midget, nursie,' protested Johnny Player, 'flap over me. I'll bet I'm bleeding like a stuck pig. Where the hell's my – oh, thanks, Sam.' He caught the round, magnifying shaving mirror that Captain Eccles had been holding for safety and gently lobbed from his already pulled out from the inner wall, Bed 18.

In their normal places 18 and 19 faced each other at the far corners of the East End and, as were the equivalents in the West, were generally occupied by the most disabled long-term bedpatients, once off the DI or SILs, since from inside far ends ran the passages off which lay the sluices, bathrooms and lavatories. As the West had the fewest beds, the EMS had converted one of its double-bathrooms into a sterilising-cum-surgical dressing room.

Mr Duncan propped himself on one of his lengthened armpit crutches to watch Johnny examine his half-lathered reflection and dab a flannel at the minute scratch on his boney chin. 'It's but a wee nick, Johnny.'

'Wee nick, my foot. Dirty great gash. Some say good old Midget – but they're getting fewer every day. Get out of my light, man! Worse than a blackout screen.'

Captain Eccles polishing his reading glasses glanced at the closed hall curtains. It was about 6.50 and it would be nearly another hour before there was enough daylight for the blackout to come down. 'We don't need those curtains now Midget's up. Bung him in the doorway and he'll do the job fine.'

'Midget' Duncan grinned amiably and moved a couple of inches.

Mr Duncan was 23 and from Aberdeen. In the summer of 1939 he had been a conscripted Militiaman, done his basic training in Scotland, and, when later sent to an Offi-cers' Training Unit, had assumed he would be commis-sioned into a Scottish regiment. On subsequently finding himself a subaltern in an English county infantry regi-ment, he had accepted the situation with an equanimity that owed as much to his temperament as to his by then sharing the ubiquitous British soldiers' conviction that the one thing to be relied upon in the Army was its bloody-minded habit of posting every man and item of equipment to the wrong place. That particular posting had resulted, last December, in his being badly wounded during one of the battles for Longstop Hill, a triple-peaked elevation a few miles from Medjez in Tunisia, regarded as vital by the British, the Americans and the Germans.

Mr Duncan thought he'd been hit on Christmas Day, but wasn't too clear of the exact date, or time, or how often and for how long he had surfaced to consciousness whilst he had lain, unable to move himself, with the battle raging backwards and forwards over his prostrate body. During his conscious periods time had become an eternity of noise, bitter, black, soaking coldness, painfully dazzling brightness, desperate thirst and agonising pain. 'They told me after I was out there but a couple of days and nights, but it was a wee bit confusing. From time to time some chap would heave up my head to pour a drink down my throat and they'd all different voices. English, Jerry, Yank – no saying who was who. When they first scraped me out the mud I'd no idea whose side was taking me in.'

MO 1 had heard this with interest and envy – one Jerry had given him schnaps – and agreed there had been nothing our chaps, those poor green Yank bastards or old Jerry could've done to shift Midget sooner as even if heavy rain had not converted the hill's soft crust to the soft mud that bogged down everyone's heavy armour, until the show was over none could've spared a tank for the job. Mr Duncan was six foot six, and when wounded, had weighed fifteen stones. In the new mid-thigh plaster on his right leg that was now nearly three inches shorter than the left, he weighed just over eleven and as he had golden hair and a very fair-skinned boyish face, he looked in dressing-gown and pyjamas a vastly overgrown, gangling schoolboy.

For the last half hour he had been helping Nurse Ashley-Ellis, the VAD relieving Nurse Kirby's nights off, to pull the beds away from the walls. Ellie came on at 7.0 and her first job was the sweeping of the whole ward. She swept this again after the patients' lunch and in the early evenings, but only for the morning sweeping were all the beds pulled out. This task, part of the night junior's 'routine', was made more difficult in MO 1 and the rest of the OU, as most of the beds were of the lowish, black iron-framed, fixed-footed type issued in Army barrack-rooms. When these beds were further weighted by patients in plasters, with fracture boards lining the bedsprings under the mattresses and iron bedcradles supporting the weight of the top bedclothes, very few nurses could move the beds alone, as was always possible if a bed had castors. If there were no up-patients well and strong enough to be allowed to help, the two night nurses allotted each ward did the beds together. In MO 1 they did this after all the bed-patients too ill to wash themselves had been washed and, if too weak to use razors, shaved, and had their dressings changed and beds re-made. When Sister arrived on duty at 7.50 the ward had to be swept, tidy, and every patient washed, shaved and in a new-made bed. The night staff were allowed to leave the six beds of their least ill patients to the day nurses who all came on at 7.30. The ward sister's appearance announced the official opening of the day, but for the night nurses this began when they 'started work' – the official term for the onset of the early morning round of washings, dressings, temperatures, bedmaking and bed-shifting that when necessary – as it usually was – began by torchlight on those patients already awake long before the main lights went on at 5.45.

It was just over two weeks from the arrival of the first Salerno-wounded and one week since Mr Dixon had been transferred to Roehampton. On the day he left, Captain Eccles had come off the SIL and been moved in his bed from SW3 to 18's place, Johnny moved across to 19, and Midget Duncan had achieved his long desire to join the kitchen crew. Three nights ago, Sergeant Pilot Kirby had completed his fifty-second op.; his station was again being temporarily rested; and Sue was spending her nights off with him in Oxford. Her relief was a newcomer to MO 1 but not to Everly Place, and had two years' service stripes on the left short sleeve of her blue cotton BRCS uniform dress.

Nurse Ashley-Ellis was a large, enthusiastic young woman in her late twenties, with a high voice. She delighted in being addressed as 'Corp', and to be 'back on nights with the chaps, Nurse Weston. Had all this last year on the medical side with the ladies, for my sins. Not that the good ladies weren't poppets to a patient, but had to keep watching my language. Frightful strain – bad as in the troops' wards – one damn from a nurse shocks the troops rigid – but everyone says officers wards are positively verbal sinks of iniquity – I say! Shouldn't say that to a Martha – frightfully sorry and all that – haven't shocked you rigid? Jolly D [decent] of you. Ready for a cuppa after your peep at Major Williams? Jolly G [good]! I'll get fell in brewing-up.'

A few minutes ago she had been needed in the West End. 'No bouncing on the sound fetlock till I get back, Mr D.,' she cautioned, bounding off. Midget smiled amiably, cast a canny eye at 20's screens, handed Sam Eccles Johnny's mirror, and dealt with his bed, as he, Midget, had two good arms and one good leg and had been the only East End up-patient since yesterday evening, when Mr Richards had become a reluctant bedpatient. (The hospital 'evening' started at 5.0 and ended at 9.0.)

Mr Richards had previously been Captain Carteret's replacement in the kitchen crew; Major Fraser and Mr Flynn had shared Major Grover's place during the few days of rest and feeding-up needed by all the ex-PWs before their operations. One by one they had become bedpatients until over the fourteenth post-op day and clear of the risks of post-operative reactionary or, later, secondary haemorrhage, present after all operations, and heightened by the nature of their wounds and previous treatments. But despite being post-ops, the swathing bandages and the sterile-towel-wrapped sandbags holding leg stumps down on beds to minimise the involuntary jerking of severed nerves, and the pain this caused, all five – as Mr Richards who had still to have his operation – looked so much younger and stronger that they were barely recognisable as the grey-faced, emaciated figures they had been on admission.

This transformation was most apparent in Captain Flynn in 16. He was proving so remarkably handsome that, inevitably, he was known as 'Errol'. Sister MO 1 was privately much relieved by his open devotion to his wife and son. 'Junior probationers are not what they were when we were gels,' she confided to her great friend, the Senior sister Tutor in the Martha's unit, 'and the VADs are always unknown quantities. Whenever possible I insist they be married, especially on nights, unless like that sensible Ashley-Ellis gel, they're the right sort.' And the Senior Sister Tutor agreed gravely that one couldn't be too careful with officers as young gels' heads were easily turned and one hadn't forgotten one's own experiences as a VAD in the Great War and What Officers' Wards Were Like. 'No – er – difficulty over Nurse Weston?' 'Good gracious, no, Sister! Far too sensible and, of course, a widow. Steadies a gel – unless she's the wrong sort and any gel that is, does not have charge of my ward by night or day.'

Mr Richards's pleasantly plain, thin face had occasioned Sister MO 1 no anxiety. She had recognised him as the right sort from his first morning when he had politely but firmly resisted her suggestion that he rest in bed all day and without much difficulty gained her permission to use the dutyroom telephone. He had first rung his parents in Northumberland, and then one of his four sisters. He was the only son and came in the middle. Two of his sisters were in the ATS; one was a WREN; and the fourth, in the WAAF. All were presently stationed south of The Wash and, with their girlfriends, flocked to visit him. MO 1 had demanded the secret of how he'd cornered the Windmill Theatre's chorus from an Italian prison camp, outwardly ground its teeth in envy and inwardly relished the prospect and the way Dick's popsies were keeping his mind off his coming chop.

For reasons officially known only to the senior nursing and medical staff, but guessed though never mentioned by MO 1, Mr Richards had been given the longest rest, time to see the uneventful recoveries from operations of his fellow ex-PWs, and the bed between Johnny Player and George Hall – who had collected an MC and this and that in the back at Alamein and been in a spinal plaster since last December and was the Bud Flanagan to Johnny's Ches. Allen. No chap between those two had a hope in hell of keeping the face straight enough to bite on the bullet.

Mr Richards was first on this morning's theatre list that, as habitually, started at 9.0 and Rose was presently giving him the last of the three skin preparations that were routine pre-operative therapy for orthopaedic operations, as opposed to the single prep. required before general surgery. He had had to turn bedpatient last evening to receive from Nurse Ames, the day staff nurse, the first and most extensive prep., as it included close shaving of a wide area round the specific site. At 10.0 last night Rose had given the second and then insisted he took his ordered sleeping tablets. He had slept deeply and late, and she had left this final prep. to the last possible moment. She would have much preferred it to wait until just before his premedication injection that was due at 7.50, but all preps. and dressings had to be finished by 7.0. It was a strict and essential OU rule that neither must be done whilst a ward was being swept or for the following half hour.

The relatively recent advent and general use of the new sulphonamide drugs that had replaced the old M and B's and their predecessor, prontosil, had proved as useful, and limited, as Joe Arden had observed to Rose on the night that for many reasons neither would ever forget. Consequently, sepsis in wounds whether violently or surgically inflicted, remained a constant danger. And whilst the widespread use of anti tetanus injections had so nearly eradicated tetanus that few nurses and doctors trained in this war had seen more than the isolated case, if that, the equally widespread anti gas gangrene injections had not yet removed the danger of wounds turning gangrenous though, in comparison with the last war, they had vastly reduced their incidence. Only reduced. So, in the OU, sepsis was the enemy that took second place only to death.

In the OU theatre and wards the battle with sepsis was non-stop; daily, the clean was re-cleaned; the spotless glass shelves of the dressing trolleys were swabbed with raw carbolic then covered with sterile towels on which were laid the sterile settings. All dressing bowls, kidney dishes and non-sharp instruments were boiled for twenty minutes before and after use; 'sharps' – i.e. scalpels, scalpel-blades, needles, and the glass barrels and plungers of hypodermic syringes were boiled for five minutes and then stored in lidded containers and covered by methylated spirits. In theatre and wards all surgical treatments were done by staff masked, gowned, and wearing sterile rubber gloves and using the stringently enforced no-touch-technique, that, as implied, meant that no preparation or part of any dressing or skin-prep must be touched with bare hands.

To ensure the correct boiling times, all the sterilising rooms were equipped with large wooden-and-glass twenty-minute egg timers for the great bowl sterilisers, and small five-minute timers for the smaller 'sharps' sterilisers. The use of masks was so omnipresent that large covered glass jars of white cotton masks stood near all ward entrances and the staff wore them over their faces or limp round their necks for most of their working hours. And as nursing etiquette insisted masks be removed when serving the patients' meals, escorting an official medical round, during ward reports, or Matron's daily round, it was a rare day or night senior that did not go off-duty with at least one mask in her dress pocket under her apron skirt. On average, the night nurses each used fourteen aprons every week and the day nurses, twelve, as they had one weekday off.

Rose, masked, gowned and gloved, clipped into the teeth of the artery forceps in her right hand a fresh sponge (small cotton wool ball wrapped in gauze), dipped it in surgical spirit and continued swabbing Mr Richards's chest. 'Sorry about the sting.'

He smiled with his lips. 'I can take it, nurse. Just.'

'That's his story, nursie.' Johnny removed his remaining lather and angled his held-up mirror to expose between the screen ends at the foot of 20 that was now about three feet behind his bedhead. 'Shouted blue murder when Nurse Ames got busy with her cut-throat.'

Captain Hall, flat on his back in his pulled out 21, falsettoed, ' "Dear me, Mr Richards, we are a ticklish gorilla! Not to worry. Soon be smooth as a baby's you-know-what!" '

Mr Richards grinned faintly, but genuinely, 'Nurse Ames has a nice mind.'

'Nurse Ames has a nice sharp cut-throat,' put in Johnny feelingly. 'Damn sight more than I can say for this blade.'

Captain Eccles lowered *The Decline And Fall Of The Roman Empire*. 'Seeing it's been hacking off East End beards all week, no bloody wonder it's as much use as garden shears.' He fingered his square, still blue chin. 'Shears would've done a better job.'

Midget lowered himself onto his pulled out, unmade bed. 'Let's ask Sister to scrounge us a pair.'

Johnny scowled at his reflection. 'If someone doesn't scrounge us more blades from somewhere, MO 1'll look like the Riff Chorus in *The Desert Song* and you can call me Harry Welchman, nursie.'

'If you like, Mr Player.' She had finished swabbing and with forceps in each hand begun gently draping the exposed left shoulder and the high, unevenly amputated and healed left arm stump with sterile towels. She saw the returned tension in Richards's face and added quickly, casually, 'What's happened to the five blades Sister scrounged from our pundits? Got them both back on cut-throats Mr Arden said last night.'

'Hell, nursie, that was early last week,' retorted Johnny. 'Now down to the last two. We've one, West End t'other. The Brig's wife is digging out her father's old cut-throat Beards, MO 1, for the use of.'

'Aren't there any blades left in England, nurse?'

'You should know, Dick,' replied Johnny before Rose could answer. ' "Is there anything I can get for you, Dickie, darling? Anything at all? Only got to ask?" ' He falsettoed, and then in his own voice went on, 'And what does he ask 'em all for, nursie? "Bring me razor blades, my own, my treasure –" he demandeth by the dozen. Hooks 'em by the battalion! Believe you me, under your soft, ministering hands right now lies a wolf with more SA in his big toe than our Errol's namesake, Robert Taylor and Clark Gable put together.'

'I believe you, Mr Player.' And thank God for you, right now. 'Just lay off a moment. You're making this wolf laugh so much he's about to choke.'

'My lips shall be sealed, nursie and –'

'He has to be joking, nurse!' chorused Mr Richards with the East End and the following shout of laughter floated over the hall and through the West End into SWs 1 and 2, and evoked a smile in Major Williams's sunken, feverish, eyes and caused the Brigadier to brush up his neat, grey moustache, as was his mannerism when gratified. And in 4, in the main body of the West End, Major Fraser nodded to himself over yesterday's *Times*. Young Dick was putting up a good show but needed all the help he could get this morning. Good type, young Johnny. Always the way of it. Get one of that type in a mess, unit, or camp, and he kept the rest up to the top line.

Lieutenant Player, in common with Midget and thousands of others had been a 19-year-old conscripted Militiaman in 1939. He had then been just under five foot ten and naturally thin. He had a neat-featured, highly intelligent and mobile face, and straight, darkish brown hair whose present length would have appalled his last CO and any RSM, but amused the Brigadier when Johnny, in a spinal carriage, was wheeled to his doorway for a chat. The Brigadier enjoyed these occasions, but in each noted with concern the etchings in the thin young face of the young body's long fight with the sepsis that continued to retard the healing of what remained of the young legs.

Johnny's left, mid-thigh stump was unplastered; his right leg, with the stump just above where his ankle had been, was in a hip spica as one of the many machine-gun bullets that had crippled him when he had been the last to crawl out of his blazing tank, had shattered his right femur-joint. For the last few months that plastered leg had been encased in a 'carpet bag' – this was a broad length of thick felt wrapped round especially offensive plasters more for the benefit of their fellows than the patient concerned, as for some merciful, inexplicable reason, patients seldom, if ever, smelt their own wounds. All carpet bags were only used once, burnt after use, and exchanged regularly. And whenever possible, patients using them were nursed out-of-doors in their beds or spinal carriages.

Though now bedridden for just over a year, Johnny's thin face had a deepish tan; he enjoyed being outside and in all seasons; unless it was raining, snowing or sleeting, he daily spent hours in the open air. The tan accentuated the small white scar over the kink in his nose made by a cricket ball in the summer of 1938 a few weeks after he had left school and when he had made his first appearance in a County Cap. The blow had only interrupted his innings long enough for the application of a cold sponge to his bleeding nose and piece of strapping over the bridge. And in the pavilion and on the wooden benches and grass verges of his county ground the spectators had congratulated themselves on watching a future All-England opening bat . . . just give the boy a year or two at the most . . . The sun had shone in southern England that summer and amnesia, as wishful thinking, comes easily to the English on holiday when the sun shines and the cricket's good.

Nurse Ashley-Ellis's large, flushed, masked face appeared between the screens at the foot of the bed. 'Frightfully sorry to spread alarm and despondency, Nurse Weston,' she stage-whispered, 'but thought you'd want to know Ellie's about to come on parade.'

'Oh, God. That's torn it. I must have another three minutes. Stall her, nurse – faint – have hysterics in the kitchen – anything – but stall her.'

'Roger, nurse! Will do!' She galloped away and the East End's exchanged glances acknowledged that whilst she would send no one's pulse up and had obviously left her mare tethered to the staff's cycle-rack outside, any nurse that after running round all night was so cheerfully willing to go single-handed through enemy lines was a hell of a lot better value than a poke in the belly from a sharp stick.

A few seconds later her high, carrying voice floated back, 'Morning, Ellie! What's the weather doing outside? . . . I say! Jolly astounding weather for November but I remember . . .'

'Heaven'll reward her if I don't.' Rose laid the final towel in position, dropped both forceps into a bowl on the lower shelf of the dressing-trolley and took from the top a two-inch gauze bandage sterilised in its wrapper. She split the wrapping paper with her gloved hands and swiftly cut off several varying lengths of bandage to tie the towels in place. She began tying and fixing each length with a huge frontal bow.

Dick Richards squinted down at his white-shrouded chest, but not at his left shoulder. 'Dead smooth.'

Rose flapped her eyelashes in mock smugness. 'Bows are my speciality, Mr Richards.' (And much easier to untie in the theatre.) 'Only three to go – oh, oh – delaying tactics overcome.'

'Wait for it!' he admonished, nearly forgetting his op. in his amusement. He was glad she was around. He liked her very much, but was relieved she wasn't his type, as had she been he'd still have been hot under the collar about his first night.

She'd been bloody sweet about that, he thought. At the time and since. When, on his first morning, the chaps had told him their nickname for her, he'd already known they had her number right. And if you added in another way, a dead smooth little number with those fascinating, white-lidded black-lashed eyes and all that shining black hair that when down must reach to her deliciously small waist.

The length of her hair and how she looked with it floating down were frequent East End speculations; another was why she hadn't remarried since Stephen Weston bought it outside Lille in May '40. Johnny had come up with that bit, Dick Richards recalled, and said he'd prised it out when she pushed him out in his pram on her last nights off. Nothing odd there. Taking Johnny on outings was something most of the MO 1 nurses did at sometime in their off duty, and he could use the breaks if any bod could. Johnny thought Snow White hadn't remarried as she hadn't had time to meet any chaps that weren't doctors and clearly didn't go for them or a Martha's chap would have hooked her years ago. Dick Richards thought that all right as a theory, but only up to a point. Bit more to it. Consciously or unconsciously, he couldn't tell which, mentally she kept a chap at arms length. That was fine and dandy if you were one of her patients, but off-putting, if you'd the mind to make a pass. As a nurse, she was the MO 1, and his, pin-up. Looked after them all like her own cherished dwarfs and had them eating out of her hand without being bossy, bitchy, or using the old nanny-knows-best line.

The nanny-types had him round the bend and he'd noticed they smarmed as often as they pulled rank, probably, he suspected, as they were constantly aware of their subservient position. Nothing subservient about Snow White, with Sister, the pundits, or the Brigadier. She was polite as hell to the lot but it was obvious to all that she would no more 'sir' a man than contemplate his preceding her through a doorway. Sam Eccles, who had a degree in law and sometimes sounded like it, said she owed this to her breeding and asked if anyone knew her maiden name as Stephen Weston's was no pointer as there were bound to be hundreds if not thousands of Westons in the gunners and in any event '40 was years back. This bit had even stumped Johnny. In fact, he hadn't opened his mouth during this particular discussion.

Poor old Johnny. Poor old Sam. Old Bill Hodges had been on the ball in the private pep-talk he'd dished out yesterday. 'Listen to me, young Dick and listen well. Hang onto the thought that you've got good legs, a good right arm and hand, and are right-handed. The tin bit'll be a bit heavy, a bit of a bind, for quite a while, but you'll get used to it and learn how to use it well. Very fine jobs of work, the tin bits they're now turning out. Your bank have kept your job open – as indeed they should – and with so many chaps away these days, promotion comes fast to those that've worked their tickets with Honourable Discharges and your stint as a PW won't hurt here, either. Nor bloody should it. Be proud of yourself, boy – you've reason to be and you'll do fine. My oath on this next bit – your premedicating injection in the ward'll make you rather sleepy and very dry, but it won't knock you out, so don't expect it to. You will be knocked flat out in seconds by your injection in the anaesthetic room and from then on you'll know nothing, I repeat, nothing, until you wake up in this bed a few hours later. You'll have another knock-out to help you through your first night, and after that you won't want or need one. We'll keep you in bed for a bit, like all the other chaps, then you'll be up and there'll be no holding you. That clear? Good boy. You'll do fine . . .'

'Morning, all!' From the hall entrance Ellie, small and stout in her pink cotton dress, wide-strapped white apron and ultra-starched white mob cap, with a broom under one arm and an old, lidless square biscuit tin containing her hoarded store of damp tealeaves under the other, gave 20's screens the look of a visiting Matron discovering a nurse doing a fan-dance on a patient's locker. 'And how, may I ask, am I to get this ward swept up afore the day nurses come on?'

'Morning, Ellie and I'm so sorry –' called Rose 'just a bit behind this morning. Done in a minute.'

'Bit behind, eh? And what am I like to be Nurse Weston, if my sweeping's not done on time and there's a queue when I get up the main kitchens for my patients' breakfast trolley? But seeing it wasn't me as made the rule no sweeping while screens is up for dressings –' she left her sentence unfinished, laid her load on the floor and folded her arms.

'Attagirl, Ellie!' Johnny blew her a kiss. 'Mutiny in the ranks, nursie. Ellie's laid down her weapons. Do what you will, I will soldier no more!'

Ellie's expression altered from outraged to dignified disapproval. Didn't do to show it, but she, for one, had a soft spot for her East End young gentlemen – proper cards and good enough for ITMA more than a few.

'I'll thank you to keep your kisses and your nonsense to

yourself, Mr Player. Weapons, indeed! No weapons allowed in no wards Everly Place as you young gentlemen well knows! But what I, for one, do not know – and if I've said it the once, Nurse Weston, I've said it the thousand times – is why you night nurses can't get done on time. Not as if you've not had all night . . .'

Her attention was diverted by the parting of the hall curtains and she enchanted the East End watchers by greeting the duffle-coated J.J. with the expression the Army termed 'dumb insolence.' 'Oh. Morning, sir.' His smiling response and immediate removal of the duffle-coat to expose his impeccably professional black jacket and pin-striped trousers mollified her automatic indignation at the sight of any doctor in her ward between 7.0 and 8.0 in the morning. Usually in Everly Place under their long white coats, Messrs Hodges and Arden wore darkish lounge suits or tweeds. Ellie liked a Proper Doctor to look like a Proper Doctor – she included no residents in this category – and regularly bewailed the passing of the pre-war custom of all Martha's honoraries of only appearing in the wards when dressed either as Mr Arden now, or in frock coats and silk stocks.

The removal of the duffle coat evoked an East End outburst of 'Stand by your bed, Midget!' 'Lie to attention, chaps!' And in the kitchen Nurse Ashley-Ellis informed a solitary cockroach that war or not war some things just weren't done and it was jolly B [bad] form for a pundit to show up unsummoned at this hour. She stamped on the cockroach, muttering, 'Frightfully sorry.'

Rose's reaction was curiosity, not annoyance. She hastily removed the screens and pushed her trolley into the hall. 'Good morning, Mr Arden. Sorry about the slight hold-up.'

He smiled as he had at Ellie and the patients.

'I must apologise for coming in, nurse – and to you, Ellie – I know I'm as welcome as hail in June. But I'm off to London and stopped in to hand over this.' He took a single, cellophane-wrapped razor blade from his wallet. 'Forgot to give it to you last night.'

The blade raised a cheer in the East End and more decorous chorus of appreciation from the West. Johnny called, 'Where'd you get it, sir? Do you have a black market and if so, name your price.'

'With you directly, Johnny.' Joe Arden turned to Rose. 'Will you tell Sister that as I've got to be in London most of today and Mr Hodges'll be tied up in the theatre all morning, the full round'll have to be this afternoon.'

'Yes, Mr Arden,' she said, as she had when he told her this last night. She was quite sure he hadn't forgotten that blade, but saved it to use as an alibi to see Richards this morning and wish him luck. Now she had come to know J.J. better, she knew this was the kind of thing he would do and liked him very much for it. She was still unsure if she liked him personally; on duty she had not had time to think upon this angle; off duty she had been too tired to think of anything. Tomorrow, she was due for her third set of nights off and up to this morning she had worked sixty-two on and had six off.

He said very quietly and without looking towards Richards, 'All well, nurse?'

She kept her back to the East End and pulled down her mask. 'Very good sleep and much better than could be expected.'

'Good.' He smiled professionally. The exhaustion in her face disturbed him so much he had to address her cap. 'Please ignore me, nurse – you too, Ellie. I'll just have a word with the chaps and then push off for my day of explaining to Medical Boards what they could read for themselves in the reports in their hands written on our ex-patients by Mr Hodges or myself.'

'You have my sympathy, Mr Arden.'

'Thanks, Nurse Weston.' He strolled into the bed-crammed middle of the East End whilst Ellie began flinging handfuls of tealeaves onto the cleared floor by the inner wall. 'Hawkins, in Avonly, Johnny.'

'Hawkins, sir? He the chemist next to the Tudor Rose, or the chap opposite? And does this mean a new lot's come in?'

'Hawkins's has, and he's the Tudor Rose side. I forgot the name of the chemist over the high street, but Mrs Hodges wasn't able to get any from him yesterday. She could only get two from Hawkins though she's a regular customer. I must hand the other into Hut 9 before I push on to London.' He paused, apparently absently at the foot of 20. 'How goes it, Dick?'

'Great, thanks, sir.'

'Aside from being bloody starving.'

A fleeting smile momentarily erased some of the tension from Dick Richards's eyes. 'I'd forgotten you'd had our eyeview on this, sir.'

'Not the identical view, lad.' He leant on the top foot-rail, and looked slowly over the odd-angled beds, then at Ellie briskly sweeping her scattered tealeaves and then at Rose, seated at the desk under the pushed-up, un-shaded light, putting the final touches to her night report in the log book. 'There were a few variations when I bought my ticket with a Blighty one. A, instead of Blighty it got me into a French Field Hospital; B, our nurses were a pair of minus C3 medical orderlies and one extremely kind but decidedly elderly nun, none of whom spoke a word of English; C, none of MO 1's other luxuries present.' He grinned and tapped himself. 'Private. PBI [Poor Bloody Infantry] and if you want my last three [digits of his old military number] I can give them to you.'

Dick Richards and the East End immediately demanded more. Rose paused in her writing without looking up. No one's ever heard him talk about his war in the OU, she thought, and it must've been such hell that it's still hell for him to remember. He's doing that now for Richards – thank God for J.J. too. She went on with her writing.

In the East End Joe Arden said, 'Sorry, chaps, have to leave it there or I'll miss my Avonly train and connection at Guildford. Some other time,' he added, knowing he had left them with a new subject to fill the conversation until 7.50.

'Can you hold it just one moment, sir? Advice wanted.' Johnny used his bedtable to haul and keep himself sitting nearly upright. 'You've given me a brainwave. Nurse Weston's pushing my pram into Avonly for coffee on Wednesday morning. If we do a blade-crawl, we might clean up. She'll ooze glamour in the chemists and I'll lie without groaning and rubbing my blue chin. Advice needed here. Should I touch up the beard with gentian violet?'

He turned back to them and for a second or two stood looking down at the thin, ill, young faces turned towards him and looking tall, straight, well-groomed and elegant as he stood amongst them. And as so often, here and in other wards, he felt guiltily aware of his own health, of the sheer luck that had allowed him to reach his present age, and to do the job he loved and that for years, until very recently, had been all he asked of life. He had never forgotten the boys that had been his friends and comrades and that had fought and died when he, another boy, had fought and lived. Most of these are not much older, he thought, and a few still have boys' faces, but none, boys' eyes. They'd to shed their boyhood prematurely to do men's jobs and what's left of their youth is now being wasted in hospital beds. He said thoughtfully, 'Not gentian for you, Johnny. Brown crayon. Got one? Not to worry, I'll bring one on tonight – no, tomorrow. Mr Hodges is on tonight.' He jerked up a thumb. 'All the best, Dick.'

'Thanks very much, sir. Have a good day in London.'

'Thanks. See you tomorrow and all of you, have a good day.' He strolled on to the desk and kept his back to the East End. 'Don't move, Nurse Weston. You're right. Taking it well. Seven-fifty!'

'Yes, Mr Arden.' She looked up at him. She was too tired to say more than was necessary but not to notice that he looked younger and very attractive in that suit and was watching her very kindly.

He murmured, 'Once again to repeat what I said last night, Mr Hodges doesn't anticipate a long job. It should all be over well before ten this morning.'

Her wide, tired eyes shone with relief. 'I hope so.'

He nodded, picked up his duffle coat and left the ward without either saying more or suspecting how this brief exchange would haunt them later.

4

Rose was taking Major Williams's sleeping pulse in SW1 and Nurse Ashley-Ellis filling dressing drums in the dutyroom, when Joe Arden came silently through the hall curtains. Seeing the red pool of light on the empty desk, he paused to look quickly around and inhale more than the tangible elements in the heavy nocturnal atmosphere. He wore a white coat over his best professional suit and his professionally impassive face looked years older than when he had left MO 1 that morning.

The only patient awake was Major Chalmers, in 10, in the far right corner of the West End from the hall. He saw the shadowy outline of the head above the half-open screen protecting the bedhead of 7, three down on his immediate left, and hauled himself up on his leather lifting straps to gesture towards SW1; and when the long white figure disappeared silently into the glowing red cavern, Major Chalmers lowered himself reflectively. Trust Johnny to know a thing or two; 6–4 on J.J. showing up out of turn as NDO [Night Duty Officer]; 10–1 Old Bill, as posted. Johnny still awake? Didn't sound like it and too dark to see. Peter Williams had the only light on the floor by his bed tonight. SWs 3, 4, and 20 – out of service. Damned bad show. Damned tough luck on – as you were, Charlie! Enough said.

Major Chalmers of the 19/23rd and Alamein-wounded, had both legs in traction, and one of the three genuine, high orthopaedic beds fitted with overhead Balkan beams suspending lifting straps that MO 1 possessed. He was a professional soldier in his mid-thirties, with a round, prematurely balding head and large black cavalry moustache and a hunting horn under his bottom pillow. He enjoyed soldiering and loved horses with the depths of passion the inarticulate harbour for their chosen objects of adoration. Alamein had finally reconciled him to the mechanisation of the cavalry. Bloody noisy show, Alamein. Sensitive creatures, horses; sensitive as some women and a damned sight more than others.

He glanced anxiously towards SW 1 though all he could see in it was the footrail of the bed. Snow White reminded him of a filly he'd once had. Same splendid mouth, nippy ankles and sensitive as they came. All eyes and white as a ghost tonight. Damned upset, but not letting it on. Knew the form. Old campaigner for all she was just a filly. Damned bad show that turn-up this morning. Bloody bad luck on young Dick – damned tough on his family – those pretty fillies – as you were, Charlie! Leave the thinking to the brainy types. Never did you any good. The old man knew a thing or two.

Major Chalmers's late father, a Classics professor, had received from his son unbounded affection, admiration and a total lack of understanding. Major Chalmers had never forgotten the faint sigh with which his father had greeted the news that he wanted to make the Army his career, nor the financial sacrifices his father had made to further this wish. Nor his, 'As you've never learnt how to think, Charles, you may well prove a most successful soldier – I trust this doesn't offend you? I assure you, that, in my view, the majority of the human race is so incapable of exercising thought or holding any opinions of intellectual worth that any attempt to exercise their minds proves as litte value to themselves as to others.' In the event, Major Chalmers had not been offended and gained the fixed belief that thinking was a bad thing unless one was a brainy type. He respected brainy types and, whenever possible, avoided their company. When circumstances forced the association, as in MO 1, he treated them with the patience – if far less understanding – that he had always shown highly-strung horses and battle-inexperienced, young troopers.

He looked across the ward to Major Fraser in 4. Glad poor old Sandy was finally having a decent kip. Took him longer than usual to get off. Same for the chaps down East, if he knew a thing or two. All that time in the same bag as – as you were, Charlie! If one's got your number on it, it's got your number on it – 'nough said – carry on S'arnt-Major – carry on, chaps – watch it! Take cover! Coming out. Lie doggo. Upset her to find you still awake after fetching you that extra cuppa before vanishing into old Peter's billet. Bad form to upset her more. Putting up a damned good show but a look at the back of her eyes tonight that upset a chap. This spot of leave for the next seventy-two was just what she needed, but a chap would miss her. Hold on – Sweet Sue back tomorrow night. Very fetching little filly – something to look forward to and a chap needed something – sometimes.

Major Chalmers closed his eyes as the two figures backed silently from SW1 and he was asleep before their slow round from bed to bed was half over.

Jill Ashley-Ellis came from the neighbourhood and lived at home. This evening she had overslept and it was 8.59 when she thrust her bicycle into the rack outside and shot across the hall in her outdoor greatcoat and pork-pie hat. She had on her indoor cap but had still to put on her apron when Rose disappeared into the dutyroom for the report. She charged into the kitchen buttoning her apron waistband. 'Frightfully sorry, Mr D.! Overslept. And you single-handed – fearfully sorry – been round to ask who wants what?'

'List's on the table, Corp. Just dealing with cocoa.'

She noticed vaguely that Midget D. wasn't quite up to his usual form, but was too sleepy to wonder if he was browned-off, or something. And then, after seeing Sister off, Rosie Weston called her into the dutyroom. 'Shut that door a moment, Corp. They're all right for a few moments. Just seen 'em. There's something I've got to tell you about the ward. Bad news, I'm afraid,' she said calmly, and gave it.

Nurse Ashley-Ellis's large, cheerful face paled. 'Dead?'

she gasped incredulously. 'Mr Richards? Honestly?'

'I'm afraid so. 9.10 this morning.'

'Just – just like that?'

'Yes.'

'But – frightfully sorry and all that, nurse, but I don't get it. This – "status lymphaticus" – that what you said?' Rose nodded, icily calm. 'What does that mean, actually?'

'Briefly, in non-medical jargon, that your body can't tolerate an anaesthetic. If you have one –' Rose snapped icy fingers 'like that.'

'But – couldn't they've known? Before?'

'No. There's no known way of telling until someone that can't take an anaesthetic gets given one. Thank God only about one in thousands – could be ten thousands – can't. I've only known of this happening once before and heard of it once somewhere else. The one I saw happened in Martha's Hut theatre last year. Identical to this morning's, from Sister's report. Nothing we could do then was any use. Hell for all concerned and the inquest doesn't help.'

'Inquest?'

'Yes.' Rose looked, sounded and felt an automaton. If I hadn't turned into one, she thought, I'd have to run straight out of MO 1 and never come back to nursing anywhere. 'There has to be an inquest when a patient dies on the table whether it's in the theatre proper or the anaesthetic room, like this morning. English law. Makes sense though it inevitably prolongs the agony for the relatives and those that have to give evidence.'

'The RA [Resident Anaesthetist]?'

'Yes. And Mr Hodges. His patient.'

'I suppose so. I say – didn't even get to the theatre?'

'No.'

'Oh, gosh, how frightful – and he was so terrified, poor chap – wasn't he?'

'Yes.' Rose flicked out her watch. 'You've only got Midget. Get those drinks out.'

'Roger, nurse,' but she didn't move. 'Er – what do I say to the chaps?'

Rose looked at her blankly. 'Nothing. They won't

mention him to you. Just ignore the empty bed and go on as usual.'

Jill Ashley-Ellis was too appalled to hide it. One knew one had to keep the old chin up and all that but somehow one hadn't expected Rosie Weston whom one had thought a jolly D senior to be – let's face it – so callous. Just calmly shrugging it off as routine. Obviously. 'I must say you are – er – frightfully unflappable about all this, nurse.'

Momentarily the automaton vanished and the truth surfaced. 'Because I've no bloody alternative.' Rose spat the words. 'Nor've you. Our job's with the living, not the dead. We can't help Dick Richards. We can and we bloody must help MO 1 so when you take first drinks round, you smile if it splits your face and natter. They won't think you cold-blooded. They'll be trying not to think at all as they know that's the only way to take this as this is something they've all had to take time after bloody time before.' She jerked a thumb. 'Every man in there has fought at least one big battle – most – rows of battles backwards and for-wards in the desert under Wavell, Auchinleck, Alexander, Monty – they've seen men – friends – die more times than they can bear to remember and die far more horribly if not more tragically than that poor boy this morning. Right now the lot are trying not to think. Some'll cope with that. Not all. The "not alls" will be easy to spot. They'll be making the most noise. Get me?'

Jill Ashley-Ellis was puce and beginning dimly to under-stand why Sue Kirby had kind of given her the impression that though a jolly D type, Rosie Weston was a bit of a dark horse. She was equally aware that 'Rosie Weston' seemed to have struck a chord that echoed back to before the war and somewhere had a wrong note. Having no time to pursue either, a second later she had forgotten those thoughts. 'Roger, nurse, but – just having another fright-ful thought. If the Eyeties had had any anaesthetics would – er –'

The automaton had returned and cut her short. 'He'd have been dead over a year. Had we only had ice and

71

cotton wool, he'd be alive tonight. Get weaving on those drinks, Corp. I must get back to them. We're quiet as hell tonight, but they've been alone long enough. You okay now?'

'Yes. Thanks.' Jill charged back to the kitchen beaming gallantly. 'Sorry to abandon you, Mr D.! Let's have another shuftee at the book of words . . .'

The whole OU was quiet tonight. The General Surgical side was moderately busy and the Medical, hectic.

'If it's not the one, it's the other,' said the Night Sister on her first round. She was a slight, dark-haired woman in her early forties with the habitually pinched expression and pink-veined nose of the chronic dyspeptic. She had been in charge at night from the opening of the EMS hospital and her successive night seniors had learnt to judge the measure of her indigestion and temper from the colour of her nose. It was a beacon tonight. 'You don't know how lucky you are in this ward, Nurse Weston. The medical nurses are being run off their feet – wards bulging with bronchials and cardiacs. It's this unseasonably warm weather. People will forget it's late November and that whatever the sun's doing the air is growing colder and the nights very cold. They will go out without coats and then, of course, catch chills they neglect that turn to pneumonia and though for most cases the sulphonamides can now clear that up in a few days, for those few they don't appear to touch, pneumonia remains the very serious illness it always was until we started using M and B 693. Prontosil helped a little, but not enough to stop more than a handful of pneumonias going through to the old ninth-day crisis, and we've a man in Medical 4 going through to that now, as nothing we're giving him is touching him. Most unfortunate about Mr Richards,' she continued without pause, 'so upsetting for the surgeons and anaesthetist.' She did pause then to click her tongue against her teeth and back into the cloak Rose was holding up. The Night Sister was neither callous nor unkind, but having literally no time for grief on duty, those tongue-clicks were her routine reaction to what was for her a routine event that occurred

72

almost nightly, and often more than once, in at least one of the many wards for which she had overall responsibility.

'Thank you, Nurse Weston.'

'Thank you, Sister.'

Half-an-hour later: 'Praise the Lord for once the OU's having it quiet. That the lot, Nurse Weston?'

'Yes, thanks, Mr Lomax.'

'Great. 'Night, nurse.'

"Night, Mr Lomax. Incidentally, Mr Hodges around somewhere?'

'Oh, God, forget my own name next.' Mr Lomax slapped his forehead. 'Should've told you the bosses've switched. J.J.'s on tonight. Packed Old Bill home for an early night. That poor sod's croaking got the old boy right under the belt. Face was the shade of his operating vest when he took off his gown after the mortuary trolley shoved off and in such a muck sweat you could've wrung out his mask. He and the RA gave the poor stiff the works. No bloody use. Goner from scratch. Bloody awful turn-up for the book, wasn't it.'

Rose looked at him blankly. 'Yes, Mr Lomax.'

Cool as a cucumber, he thought, being too shaken by this morning in the anaesthetic room, and too tired to think in anything but clichés, and too inexperienced to see more than the composure in the face of the nurse the Everly Place housemen rated the biggest little Ice Cold Katy in the frozenmitt business and wrote off so finally that only the two orthopaedic housemen ever troubled to speculate amongst themselves how her husband ever thawed her enough to bed her, and with such little interest that neither they nor their colleagues had yet discovered she was a widow.

'If that's all I'll push off and make history by getting to bed by midnight for the first time since I arrived in this dump.'

'I hope you do and don't get called-up, Mr Lomax.'

They came slowly from the dark East End into the lighter, red-tinged darkness of the hall and stood at the desk. He glanced at her face and then into both ends. 'Your junior handy, Nurse Weston?'

73

She looked up in surprise. 'Doing her routine in the outhouses, Mr Arden. You want her?'

'Could she watch the ward whilst we have a word outside?'

Of course, she thought heavily, the time of the inquest. I should've guessed, were I not half-zombie. He won't want to discuss this at the desk. Someone might wake and see us and most've been in long enough to lip-read. 'I'll get her.'

He looked back at her. 'Thanks'.

When he had first returned to doing night rounds a few weeks ago, he had found the darkness of the wards half-blinding, but having in the past spent a dozen years walking the wards at night, old habit had swiftly reasserted itself and he could now see nearly as well in the dark as Sergeant Pilot Kirby, whose night vision was the envy of his fellow pilots and relief of his crew and Wing Commander.

Rose slid round the screen covering the lighted passage doorway and as the kitchen was empty hurried on to the dutyroom. 'Sorry to break in, Corp. J.J. wants a private chat. Could you watch the ward, please. They're all okay, but keep an eye on Major Williams. Pulse is up a bit.'

'Roger, nurse.' Jill came into the passage shedding fragments of gauze and cotton wool. 'If J.J. wants a cuppa, masses of char in the blue caddy. Sister doubled our ration tonight. Don't know why.'

'Thanks.' And if you don't know why, thought Rose, you don't know Sister, and I've neither the time nor energy to put you wise right now. Not just Richards though I could weep for him and his family. I'm always half-zombie on my last night before third nights off and have to concentrate to keep my eyes open and daren't lean against the back of a chair or wall, or I'll be asleep. Not that Joe Arden'll want a drink – he never does, she decided, without noticing the wording of that decision. But, my God, am I glad he's here tonight and not Old Bill – a sweetie – but when upset over a patient whoffles on and on about golf and making corny jokes about the rattling good chaps in the trenches and if I had to take that tonight as I'm so sorry for him too I'd probably burst into tears on him. She glanced down then quickly away from her spotless apron bib as she went back to the hall. Only just over two weeks ago . . . Back. Safe. Home soon.

'Dutyroom, Mr Arden?'

'Kitchen.' He waited for her to precede him and then went straight over to investigate the hot water urn on the cooker. 'On the boil. Good. What's your tea situation tonight, nurse?'

My God, he's got something hideous to tell me, she thought, and gave the back of the white coat floating from his wide shoulders a look of defeat that only a few of her set but none of her professional seniors or juniors or her patients had ever seen in her brown eyes. 'We've plenty tonight.' She took a small teapot and the blue caddy from the dresser. 'I'll make some.'

'Let's have them.' He took both from her and glanced round the steamy, reeking kitchen. 'No chair. Right. Sit on the table.'

She blinked, wondering if she had heard right. 'Table, Mr Arden?'

'Yes.' He gave her a long, openly clinical look. 'Sit on it. If you nod off, you'll wake up falling off.' He spoke quietly, even lightly, but there was no disguising the order. 'You can soothe your very correct sense of etiquette with the reflection that I was brewing-up before you were born.'

She obeyed mechanically and feeling suddenly so light-headed that she half-wondered if she had fallen asleep and was dreaming. 'You mean in the last war?' He nodded without looking up from his search for a teaspoon in the cutlery drawer. 'Until I heard you talking to the East End this morning I thought you'd been in the RAMC with Mr Hodges.'

He looked up and smiled faintly and self-derisively. 'No. PBI.'

'So you said.' The relief of being off her feet had aroused a longing for sleep of tidal wave proportions. She fought it down. 'How long were you in?'

'Tail end. Time my lot got to France the last Spring

Offensive was nearly over. MO 1 out of teaspons?'

'We should have three somewhere. I'll –'

'Stay put, nurse. A dessert'll do.'

She widened her eyes to keep them open. I must keep talking, she thought, I must, or I'll be flat out. 'Spring Offensive of '18?'

'That was the last one.' He made the tea and set the pot on the table to brew. 'If you must drop off, drop to your right and you'll hit table not floor. Good size table. Plenty of room.'

Her fight with sleep jolted her into night-nurses' euphoria and she smiled foolishly. 'I will, Mr Arden.'

He glanced over his shoulder as he took a quart bottle of milk from the refrigerator, and only long experience enabled him to contain his anger at the appalling hours and constant hard work demanded of the night nurses. This had often angered him before, but never to this extent, and the sight of that uncharacteristically foolish smile on her grossly overtired face told him precisely why, and disturbed him, profoundly. He said evenly, 'Good.'

Rose's euphoria shot into the chatty stage. 'My father was killed in that last Offensive – April '18 – five months before I was born. He was 25 like Stephen – oh, sorry, you won't know who he was – my husband – a gunner – Lille, 29 May, '40 – like Mr Richards –' she rattled on without noticing the care with which he put the milk bottle on the table 'no – that's wrong. Mr Richards was 24 – I'm mixing him up with Captain Eccles – no, that's wrong – Captain Eccles in 28 and much the oldest in the East End though some of the others are married and he's not – I suppose that's a good thing – like Mr Richards – I don't know – but that wasn't what I meant to say. I meant to say, like me now. I'm 25 – that's quite old for this war – I expect it was quite old for your war, wasn't it? How old were you in '18?' Suddenly she heard herself and her euphoria turned off like a tap. 'I'm so sorry, Mr Arden. I'm talking nonsense and I shouldn't have asked that.'

'That's all right, nurse.' He had found the sugar, added two dessert-spoonfuls to the mug he had just filled with tea, stirred it with the spoon's handle and pushed the mug towards her. 'Drink up. Your blood sugar can use it. How old was I then? Seventeen, plus, when my unit got to France. I wasn't the youngest on either side.'

She was thankful for the tea and that it was so hot that she had to sip it, which gave her a breathing space to collect her scattered thoughts and recover from the shock of discovering his real age. He was much younger than she'd assumed or he looked, she thought and then corrected herself. No. All he was, was much younger than she had thought he looked during the time when she had never bothered to look at him properly and so had missed the humour and kindness in his face and his remarkably sweet smile when he smiled properly. He wasn't smiling now. He was watching her as he watched the patients when they were asleep or unconscious. And he wasn't drinking tea.

'Aren't you having any?'

'No, thanks. This is my last ward, then I'm going to bed. Tea could keep me awake.'

That brazen excuse from a doctor in a ward at night aroused her sense of humour and sent soaring her gratitude, respect and liking for him. Her grandparents had died within months of each other shortly after her marriage in 1938; her only living relatives were in-laws, and she couldn't at this moment recall when anyone had last shown such solicitude for her personal welfare. This isn't for what I'm worth, she thought. This is because I'm zombied.

Her eyes laughed at him. 'Forgive the corn, Mr Arden, but shouldn't you tell that one to the Marines?'

His smile was downright paternal. 'Possibly, Nurse Weston. Knock back that mug and have another. Improving your colour already.' He leant against the dresser, his hands in the pockets of his white coat. 'How many nights have you now done?'

She thought a moment. 'Sixty-three tonight. That's why I'm a zombie.' She explained this, then added, 'After third nights off I get my second wind. This varies for night nurses. Some get it after the first month. I get it in my last and then feel I can go on indefinitely. I wouldn't be such a zombie tonight if we were hectic. I can always wake up when we are, but being quiet makes it worse.'

'Invariably.' He saw the tea had revived her mind and returned the shadows to her eyes. He had to shift them, if only temporarily. 'Sleep well, on nights?'

'Fine, thanks.'

He frowned. 'I don't want a placebo, nurse. The truth.'

'Fine, is true.' Being no longer light-headed, she saw he no longer looked paternal. He looked now, she thought, as punditish as his suit. And unconvinced. 'Honestly, Mr Arden. Once in bed I'm so flat out not even another direct hit would wake me.'

'Another?' he echoed casually.

She was only a little surprised to hear herself telling him about the PTS in 1940 even although it was not a subject she had ever discussed outside of her set. And hearing herself, she thought, the escalators have stopped again.

Ever since the summer of 1940, in and out of hospital, she had had the sensation of being permanently on one rung of a temperamental escalator that ran parallel with another of similar eccentricity. At some times both ran up, down, or in opposite directions at the same rate; at others, one ran faster than the other, or one stopped whilst the other moved on, or, and always briefly, they stopped simultaneously. Then, in those short stops, she had discovered herself forming close relationships with strangers in hospital wards, hospital beds, on Tube platforms in use as air-raid shelters, and in the carriages and corridors of trains held up outside towns, cities and stations under air attack until the all-clear sounded ahead. In all those times, the omnipresent awareness of shared danger had evoked the shared laughter, tears and type of personal revelations that all, in peacetime, would have hesitated to share even with lifelong friends. And, always before there was time for regrets or even embarrassment, the escalators jerked in opposite directions to mutual cries of . . . nice meeting you . . . see you around, sometime . . . take care of yourself . . . cherrio . . . cheers. Never 'goodbye' she'd noticed. No one seemed to say 'goodbye' in this war, probably as two generations had learnt what that word meant. And then, again, before there was time to wonder what had happened to him or her in the last stop, the escalators made another, and there were new faces on the parallel rung, new shared dangers, emotions and confidences, and very shortly, inevitably . . . nice meeting you . . . see you around, sometime . . . take care . . . cheers.

Joe Arden watched his feet whilst he listened and when she finished speaking he didn't look up at the sweet, tired Dutch doll's face that for these last couple of weeks had haunted his mind. 'Martha's has copped more than her share. Benedict's had been damned lucky. Just over the river but no worse than busted windows and cracked ceilings.'

Rose tapped the table. 'Please don't tempt Jerry.'

His head jerked up and as their eyes met he saw that she too was wincing at the memory of their final exchange this morning. 'You're right not to blame Providence for the actions of men, nurse. Too handy an alibi.'

She said quickly, 'If anyone needs an alibi for Richards's death, it's Jerry for starting this war. He was a civvy soldier. If he'd been able to live his life in peace he might never have needed an anaesthetic. Thousands, don't.'

Her insight and honesty touched him like a gentle handclasp. 'That's true, but doesn't alter the fact that he was our responsibility. What happened wasn't our fault, but others got him safely back to us and – we lost him.'

'I know, Mr Arden.'

'Yes.' He had to drag his eyes from her face. 'I'm very sorry. Right.' He backed to the door. 'I'll see myself out. Have another mug before you go back to them. Oh – one item I've forgotten – tell Sister MO 1 I had time to get into Benedict's today and do some plain talking that may get us a registrar in the next week or two.'

'I'll tell Sister. I hope you get one. Doing without is putting a tremendous amount of extra work on you and Mr Hodges.'

'A bit tricky. However, as I was reminded ad nauseam in Benedict's today, down here in our quiet little backwater out of the war, we've obviously forgotten there's a war on.'

She flushed faintly with indignation for him. 'How did you answer that?'

'Unrepeatable to your sex, Nurse. 'Night.'

'Goodnight and thank you very much for the tea,' she said to his back. He raised a hand in reply but didn't look round. She watched the empty doorway until she heard the swish of the hall curtains, then she topped up her mug and took it into the hall.

'Thanks, Corp. I'll take over. How've they been?'

'All quiet on Western and Eastern Fronts, nurse.'

'Good. There's a cuppa going in the kitchen. Help yourself.'

'Jolly G! I say – J.J. turning human?'

'Why not?' Rose put the mug on the desk and picked up her torch to go all round her sleeping ward. 'He is.'

5

'Razor blades, miss?' From the woman's expression she
had been asked for black market whisky, but her tone
was deferential. She was the widowed daughter of Mr
Hawkins, the owner-cum-dispenser of the oldest chemist
in Avonly, and had been born in the front bedroom over
the little shop her grandfather had installed in his front
parlour and recognised carriage trade when she saw it.
Her sharp eyes noted that her sole customer's belted
camel-hair coat, leather gloves, handbag and brogues had
seen a bit of wear – whose hadn't these days? – but all
good quality and nothing on her face but the touch of
powder and lipstick and her black hair done up ladylike.
This wasn't one of those tarted-up no better than they
should be bits of fluff down from London after the Americans. 'I wish I could help out, miss, but my old dad'll not
hear of it. Regular customers only, he says, and just the
two. I'm ever so sorry.'

Plan A or Plan B? Rose glanced around the little shop
that smelt of cough mixtures and the wax polish on the
high, old-fashioned mahogany counter and that, even on
this bright morning, was dim. The one small bay window
was blocked by huge bottles of red, yellow and green
liquid and the strips of anti-blast paper criss-crossing the
leaded panes. The panes in the door that had an overhead,
jangling bell, were blocked by black paper and as the door
had been shut when she came in she had closed it after her.

The woman misinterpreted Rose's glance. 'Ever so patri-
otic, my old dad, miss. Won't waste electricity daytimes
and no use telling him Avonly's not had the one raid yet.

That's as may be, he says. Got to remember there's a war on, he says.'

Rose reacted as if hearing this for the first time. 'Your father's Mr Hawkins, I presume? He's so right and this is exactly why –' and she launched into Plan A, that, as B, Johnny had outlined to her in the winding lane and which ended with '. . . if you can possibly spare one or two the whole ward will bless you.'

'Oh, dear, oh, dear, miss.' The woman's worn, tight-lipped face had creased in sympathy. 'I don't like to disappoint the poor wounded gentlemen, I'm sure, but I know my old dad once his mind's made up.' She looked over her shoulder at a darkly curtained recess behind the counter. 'All ours, would they be, miss?'

Rose had slept for twenty-five hours and had Johnny not revealed so much more to her in the lane, that faint scent of victory would have had her resisting the temptation to sing 'There'll Always Be An England'. She said gravely, intentionally, 'Oh yes. All ours and most are Eighth Army.'

'You don't say, miss! I'll just have a word with dad – if you'll not mind waiting?'

'Not at all and thank you.' And every Desert Rat for making the Eighth the one British Army to have become a cherished household name in the UK.

It had been 10.0 before she woke this morning and she had been forty minutes late for Johnny. She rang Sister MO 1 within minutes of waking.

'I'll explain to Mr Player, nurse. His lunch will be kept hot and you need not return him until one, but no later. He must have the full rest period before this afternoon's visiting time.'

'We won't be late, Sister. How lucky it's another lovely day.'

'But much colder. He'll be well wrapped. Thank you, nurse.'

Johnny's outings to coffee in the Tudor Rose were now as established a feature of MO 1 life as the aged Morris

Oxford, the only Avonly taxi, that ferried sufficiently mobile, semi-convalescent up-patients to and from the Crown in the early evenings. No 'ups' had needed encouragement into joining the taxi outings, but it had initially taken all Sister's considerable powers of tactful persuasion to coax Johnny into allowing his crippled body to be wheeled beyond the grounds of Everly Place. He remained adamant about allowing only nurses to escort him.

'Understandably,' had said Sister MO 1 in the dutyroom when Rose first offered her services here before her previous nights off. 'Helpless young men remain young men with young men's instincts. No man of any age, and especially in youth, with any spirit, enjoys demonstrating his helplessness, and particularly not to those dear to him. Most unfortunately his mother, a well-intentioned, anxious, devoted but simple woman suggested she "take him for little walks just as she used to in his pram." ' Rose had winced. 'Yes, nurse. Relatives will say these things. I'll admit I was thankful she wasn't his wife. That remark was just pardonable from a mother; unpardonable from a wife. One or two of the young women that occasionally visit him have offered to take him out and been turned down by Mr Player – to my relief as I would have had to have done the same. Wheeling his spinal carriage damands understanding and strength. I'm not questioning your understanding, nurse, but being on night duty, will you have the energy? And are you sure you don't wish to go away for your break?'

'Quite sure, Sister. My in-laws are very hospitable, but most live in Durham. The trains are so slow and packed I'd probably spend two days travelling sitting on a corridor floor. If I take him on my second morning I'll have slept the clock round twice and have masses of energy.'

'Very well, nurse. Splendid. Nurse Ames is taking him out on Saturday so that's two for him to look forward to. I must now see what can be done for next week.'

'Shall I ask my set, Sister? Quite a few of us stay down for nights off.'

'Name them, please, nurse.' And after Rose had done

so, Sister approved of four, but not the fifth. 'A good nurse but no idea of time. Always late. To keep anyone waiting upon a social occasion is bad manners, but to keep a patient waiting upon an outing is as unkind as keeping a child waiting. Both immediately imagine themselves forgotten. Don't mention this to her, but yes, please, see what you can do with the others.'

Those four nurses had now officially joined Johnny's unofficial rota. Yesterday morning, before Rose went off, Sister confided her wish to form a similar rota for Captain Eccles. 'Though he is still against the idea, I'm hoping Mr Player's patent pleasure in his outings will eventually bring Captain Eccles round. Of course, any day now the weather's bound to cancel all outings until spring, but we must do what we can whilst we can. Have you yet heard which set'll be replacing yours on night duty, nurse?'

'Yes, Sister. The set just below ours that's presently in St Martha's, London. They're on day duty. Night Home Sister expects they'll take over from us on night duty here when we come off in the week before Christmas and that we may well spend the rest of our training in London.'

Sister MO 1 inclined her impressively capped head without comment, but as Rose knew her well, later at the seniors' table at breakfast she announced that were she a betting woman she'd put her shirt on their still being on nights over Christmas. 'I hope we are.' Her set agreed with that and her rider not to mention this to their patients in case Jerry or the Second Front that everyone kept saying was coming, decided otherwise.

Rose's arrival on her bicycle and out of uniform was greeted by a barrage of wolf-whistles from the four East Enders whose beds had been lifted out onto the ten foot wide stone ledge that, on either side of the stone entrance steps and cement ramp, ran the length of the front of the villa. The ledge stood about four feet above the ground, and on it were Captains Eccles and Hall, Lieutenant Withers, RA in a spinal plaster since his return from Sicily, and

Lieutenant Dawson, of a Guards' regiment that had fought with Midget's – and very probably over his wounded body – on Longstop Hill. Mr Dawson was in a double hip spica.

Johnny's spinal carriage was braked parallel with the ledge to face the main entrance and when Rose leapt from her brakeless bicycle and swung it into the wooden rack against the West End side of the ledge, he took off and waved his old service cap like an excited schoolboy. 'Didn't I say our nursie wouldn't stand me up, chaps!'

He was in one of the old-fashioned – and according to the patients far more comfortable than the new – carriages, that looked like a wicker sofa with low sides and foot panel on four bicycle wheels. The high, curving back rest was padded with pillows; hot water bottles were tucked between the layers of loose rugs over which was a long red rubber undersheet topped by a soft scarlet blanket. The undersheet was there as a protection against unexpected rain. If rain was forecast or falling, or it was just misty, no patients in plaster were allowed outside. When this was possible, the most crippled preferred the old spinal carriages to beds, as the former were well-sprung and being relatively light to manoeuvre gave their occupants a fractionary sensation of the mobility for which, secretly and constantly, they desperately longed. Another advantage to the users and pushers of those carriages in Everly Place was that the lane and Avonly were in low-lying land and the only incline was on the run down to and up from the main entrance.

Johnny wore three sweaters over his pyjama jacket, a red and white polka-dotted cravat, and his Army greatcoat buttoned to mid-chest with the skirt folded back and spread over the pillows behind his shoulders. The loose folds of the rugs hid his missing feet and left leg, but not the bulky outline of the stiffened folds of the carpet bag arranged to serve as a makeshift bedcradle over his plastered right leg. His appearance caught Rose by the throat. In the ward lights at night, his tan made him seem almost healthy in comparison with his paler fellows, but in the clear morning sunshine, the frailty of long illness, of weeks of pain, months of acute discomfort and the youth of his thin face were so exposed that he looked a sick boy, dressed for fun in his father's old uniform that was far too big and heavy for him.

'Hi, gentlemen! Sorry I'm late, Mr Player. Sister explain?'

'She did, nursie. All is forgiven. So what if you're playing hard to get? Big-hearted Johnny, that's me!'

The quartet boo-ed softly as Sister had appeared at a ward window to acknowledge and dismiss Rose with a regal wave. 'Bloody nurses' pet! Bloody favouritism! What's the sod got that we haven't got?'

Johnny slapped on his cap. 'SA, charm, beautiful brown eyes – what've I left out, nursie?'

She kicked free the carriage brakes. 'No oil painting but a fascinating monster?'

He laughed. 'Just you wait till I show you my etchings. Cheers, you poor, lonely, unloved, sods!'

'And a kick in the bracket to you, chum,' they retorted laughing.

George Hall added, 'Don't bother to bring him back, nursie. Tip him out in the lane but come back yourself with or without blades –' and he began singing, with the other joining in, 'You'll Never Know Just How Much I Love You' transposed into the third person plural.

Rose laughed with them, and thought, Monday morning. Today's only Wednesday. No one seeing us now would believe Monday had happened. As it did, even Sam Eccles is singing. All this bunch are civvy soldiers, but soldiers long enough to have caught the Army's habit of playing a quick march when marching back from a soldier's funeral.

She called cheerfully, 'Why has no one told me I'm nursing the Ink Spots? Thanks a lot, be seeing you, and if Avonly has blades, we'll get 'em.' She took a firm grip on the handlebar and wheeled Johnny away.

He muttered, 'Right pair of mugs we'll look if we draw a blank.'

She looked down at him quickly, then leant back to use

her shoulder and back muscles against the incline rather than a gentle pressure on the brakes that when half-on unavoidably caused a slight vibration. 'I repeat, if they're to be had, we'll get 'em. Period.'

'Skip the patter, Rosie. You're not on duty now.'

'Nor yet out of the grounds, Mr Player.'

'Christ. If I didn't know you better I'd say you were as sold on the book as Night Sister. She nearly went round the bend when I told her Sister MO 1 had given me permission to skip the shave this morning. Your relief was already round it. Round it all night though as nights go – when you're off – wasn't too bad.' He tilted his cap to a guardsman's angle and the peak nudged his nose. 'Didn't stop Flappy Flossie flapping. Sweet Sue soothed us down East with buckshee scrambled eggs and said if she was stuck with F.F. as permanent senior, she'd re-muster to the WAAF.'

There was a compassionate concern in Rose's eyes that she had never let him see, or suspect. She said casually, 'I haven't seen her since she got back. How'd her nights off go?'

'Wizard, she said. The beloved Michael prized a forty-eight out of his Wingco and if he got back in one piece this morning that'll be only seven to go before grounding. If he makes it, he wants her to try for a nearer posting and as there are hospitals all over the bloody country and she's due off nights before Christmas, could be, come Christmas, Everly Place'll see her no more.'

'Everly Place'll miss her.' She had to stop the carriage for a hospital ambulance turning in through the gateless entrance from the lane. The gates, with all the iron fencing on the estate, had gone in one of the scrap metal collections in 1940. The ambulance driver waved to them and as his machine crawled by, shouted, 'Off on the spree again, Mr Player?'

'Where else, Brian? You know me,' Johnny shouted back and when the ambulance passed he added in a very different tone, 'All know me. Straight ahead Cas. and Main Block, fork right for the Doctors' Hut. Sharp right, huts. Sharp left, Medical Blocks. Straight up and first right fork, Mr Player. Sees 'em come, sees 'em go, does Mr Player. When will I see you go, Rosie.'

They had turned into the lane and the deal they had made about using Christian names during their previous outing, came into force. 'I'm not sure, Johnny. My set's due off nights before Christmas, but –'

'Christ, no! Not you gone by Christmas –' He broke off hearing the pain in his voice and pretended to laugh. 'Sucker for old familiar faces and old socks hanging around at Christmas, am I. But if you gotta go, you gotta go.'

'We may stay on. Depends on the war.'

'There's an original thought.'

'Pipe down, clot! You know I mean it depends on who's having a flap, where. No flap anywhere, like now, with Martha's, London and Martha's Hut being able to admit "cold cases" for the first time in years, my set may well do an extra three months down here and we're all hoping so as we've Hospital Finals in January and who wants a change with – hold everything. Heavy stuff coming.' She eased the carriage gently onto the verge of the lane and held out her arms as the first of the two oncoming US Army lorries appeared round the bend ahead. The driver, standing on clutch and brakes, signalled to the one behind whilst she jumped aside and stood with her back to the roadside of the carriage. The lorries crept by, the drivers and their mates grinning and waving and the soldiers crammed into the lorry-backs exploding into wolf-whistles, catcalls and bellows of 'Jeez, Lootenant, you sure can pick 'em!' Rose knew that had she been alone they'd have bellowed, 'Hi, babe! How's about you and me?' or, 'Honey, you are the most!' or 'How's about you and I meeting up down the good old Crown, lady? Just you and me and the night and the music, lady – gee, lady – please, lady – I speak real good English too, lady – how's about it?'

Johnny, grinning, jerked up a thumb. Rose, smiling and waving, mentally blew both lorries kisses. It had been more than Johnny's rank that had restrained those GIs attempts to date her that they'd have made had she been twenty years older and looked like the back of a bus. They're lonely young men a long way from home, she thought, and they know, as ours know, their only ticket home is to be too severely wounded to fight again. Even Shakespeare had this wrong – at least, about fighting men. The only soldiers, sailors or airmen she had ever known jeer at the wounded, or wounds, had been the wounded.

She crouched to release the brakes to give Johnny the few seconds privacy he needed to recover from the sight of those friendly, healthy, young soldiers. Wheeling on, she said, 'Those Yank drivers are slipping. Corners on all four wheels.'

'Nothing amiss with their hormones.' His cap was tilted to the tip of his nose. 'Odd thing, lust. Tell me, Rosie, why is it right and proper for all red-blooded Englishmen to lust by night but only permissible for a dago or a heel to lust by day?' He didn't give her time to answer. 'So I'm a heel.'

'Only because you're in the British Army. If you were a Yank you'd be considered a blot on your outfit if you weren't lusting throughout the twenty-four hours.'

'So I would.' He brightened a little. 'Maybe I've got Yank blood? Think I could swing it on the pundits? Gee, sir –' he switched into an American accent acquired from his boyhood's addiction to the talkies 'I guess I have this real problem so I guess you will not object to my going AWOL from good old MO 1 seeing what you folks right here in Brave Little Britain owe the good old Stars and Stripes such as Lease-Lend –'

'Bundles for Britain!'

'Fifty good old – and sure as hell do I mean old – destroyers –'

'Good old Franklin D.R.!'

'Good old powdered eggs and orange juice!'

'Good old GI Joe!'

'Good old gonorrhoea!'

'Don't be unpatriotic, Johnny.' She was firm. 'We had it

first. Picked it up on the Crusades and've had it ever since. Columbus just took some over and the GIs have just brought some back. Lease-Lend working both ways.'

He shouted with laughter and pushed up his cap. 'Your round, Rosie! I'm back on balance. Get fell in behind Augustine, Johnny!' He crossed his arms on his chest. 'Celibates, look to your fronts! Sound tip. Lots to be said for celibacy. Look where it's got J.J.,' he added off-handedly.

She slowed to take another bend and queried as off-handedly, 'He's got fell in behind Augustine?'

'Marker.'

'Where in hell did you get that gen?'

'Where in hell do you think? Me. The old eyes and ears of MO 1 and Everly Place. See all and hear all in the East End, on the ledge, or in this bloody pram of a sunny morn. If J.J., or come to that Old Bill, had laid one finger on a nurse or tried to smuggle one popsie in through the back door whilst Ma Hodges was out, someone would've tipped me off. Someone always tips me off. If it's not one of the chaps or their visitors, it's a nurse, or a porter, or a chap from Repairs and Works, or a chap collecting up pig buckets, or his mate on the dirty dressing bins, or a boiler-man, or one of the ambulance crews, or a houseman, or our Ellie, or the elderly party doling out religious pamphlets, or the newspaper boy, or a padre, or you-name-it and they all stop by for a natter and dole it all out.'

She glanced up at the bare branches of the trees that had shed their remaining leaves in last night's first frost, at the dark green umbrellas of the pines and the gentle blue sky beyond. The bright sun had no real warmth and in the shadow of the trees the air on her face that was faintly flushed by the effort of pushing, was infinitely colder than yesterday's and announced that, quietly and unnoticed, winter had arrived. 'You don't dole it all out, Johnny.'

He twisted his head to her. 'If I did, I wouldn't hear all.' He faced frontwards. 'Tough luck, Mrs J.J. buying it with diphtheria.'

He was a good actor, but her sex and upbringing had

made her the better and taught her the advantage in any act, of sticking as close as possible to the truth. 'I didn't know that. When did she get dip.?'

'Early '39 from the inside gen I had from Nigel Thomas before that clot Lomax pushed Nigel up to SOH [Senior Orthopaedic Houseman] and you came into our lives. They'd only been married about eighteen months after being engaged five years.'

'Five?' She didn't try to hide her surprise. 'Why so long?'

'He couldn't afford to marry her sooner. His old man died a couple of years after he qualified and either forgot, or couldn't afford to provide his widow with a pension. J.J. had to support his mother, two sisters and himself on the couple of hundred quid a year he'd inherited from some relative and what he earned, which was damn all for years. The clot Lomax gets thirty bob a week now. At his stage J.J.'ll have been lucky to collect ten bob a week. Nigel Thomas said even when he climbed higher up the medical ladder he wouldn't have got more than three hundred a year in the '30s. His sisters took time to get themselves spliced and off his financial back. Both married before he did, and a month or so after the honeymoon his mother packed it in with pneumonia so at last he could be said to have been in the clear with just a wife to support. Very pretty very nice little thing, Nigel said, but he got that second hand from Old Bill. All in the distance by the time Nigel met J.J. Nigel didn't know where she'd picked up the dip. but could've been anywhere, he said.'

She was shocked and distressed and hid neither. Johnny had been her patient for sixty-three nights and knew her nearly as well as she knew him. 'That's right. Dip.'s endemic in London and most cities. She could have picked it up visiting him in Benedict's – the odd cases are always coming into Martha's London as acute tonsilitis or Vincent's Angina until they're diagnosed and moved on to fever hospitals – but she could as easily have caught it in any crowded bus, Tube or shop. The poor girl. How hideous for both – especially after having to wait all those years.'

He twisted his head to look up at her and said brusquely, 'Wouldn't shake you rigid over that wait if you'd ever had to count the pennies. My folks had to wait nearly three years for the old man to afford a wife. Those revoltingly corny posters the government shoves up everywhere, "BE LIKE DAD, KEEP MUM," apply to roughly ninety-nine percent of British marriages.' He saw what he was doing to her and was stricken with shame and so sounded more brusque. 'Scrub that guilty blush, Rosie! Not your fault you've never needed an umbrella for more than the trip down the front steps to the door of the Rolls the chauffeur's holding open. Just your bloody good luck in having a grandfather with the brains to come up with the idea – and nous to patent it – for the rifle that from my old man's account – and he used one from '15 to '18 – did as much for the home side as the longbow did for the English yeomen at Crécy, Agincourt and Flodden.'

Rose's colour had drained. 'How do you do it? I didn't know anyone –'

He cut her short. 'Apart from me, they don't. I didn't get this from Everly Place. Just in it.'

'When? How?'

'Hold everything. Where are we now?' He lay back and looked up at the sky through the pines. 'End of November. Yes. Just after your last nights off. Remember me telling you my old CO paid me a visit?'

'Yep. He tell you my nickname at school was Trigger? Trig to my chums?' she demanded bitterly.

'No. Shut up and listen. We'd run out of the small talk as one always does once over the "You're looking fine, old chap, sure you've got everything you need, old chap" routine, so for something to say he said it was too bad Somerset was a bit far off for my folks' visits and that I wasn't from Surrey, Hampshire or Sussex but preferably Sussex old chap as he was a Man of and so on. Purely to fill the gap I said both night nurses were Sussex types, and a bit about the Kirbys and then you and your late. He stiffened as if I'd stuck a ticking bomb under his chair, but being an old sweat didn't give much away. He did say from the dates your Stephen Weston must have been the one that was a pal of his son's at The Shop and that Stephen's buying it was a bad show but no chap had all the luck and that he had heard young Mrs Stephen was nursing in one of the big places and thought that a jolly fine show in her circumstances. As, by then, I was bloody curious, I asked, what circumstances. He told me.' He paused but she kept silent. Then, 'If it's any comfort, and it bloody should be, he shares my old man's views on your grandpappy's brain-child.' Again, he paused, and she said nothing. 'Right. Tip the sod out of the pram and have done.'

'No.' She steadied the carriage with one hand and with the other removed his cap and lightly ruffled his hair. 'No sod. Saint Johnny, that's you.'

He tilted back his head sharply and glared up into her troubled face. 'Don't you bloody believe it!' His eyes blazed and his voice vibrated with anger, frustration and passion. 'If I'd my bloody feet, whole legs and a bloody hope and you weren't so bloody sweet and so godamn bloody awful rich – but I haven't and you are, so bloody shut up and let's get cracking on our pincer attack on Avonly! I've worked out Plan A and Plan B. I tried them on the chaps this morning. Try 'em on you now and if you don't buy 'em you can bloody come up with Plan C – and keep your hands off me! And get this, Snow White! My name is Henry Arthur Player known as Johnny, but *not*, repeat, *not* Dopey. So you don't have to tell me you don't bloody love me. I know it. Just as I know you know I bloody love you like hell but as there's damn all I can do about it, forget it! Loud and clear?'

She was too near tears to look up from the handlebar. She nodded and in her most detached voice, said, 'Let's have the Plans, Johnny.'

Mr Hawkins preceded his daughter from the curtained recess. He was white-haired and wiry with steady eyes, a slow countyman's voice, and the third and fourth fingers of his right hand missing. 'My daughter's explained, miss and I do see how you're placed, but I've only the dozen left and all promised to my regulars. I can't let my regular customers down, miss.'

Rose murmured sympathetically, registered the missing fingers, and switched to Plan B. 'May I show you some-one, Mr Hawkins?' She backed and opened the door with-out waiting for an answer. Four narrow stone steps led up from the pavement to that door and the carriage was drawn up against the lowest step. The jangling bell alerted Johnny. Attagirl! Plan B. He delivered the brave smile and weak salute he had practised in his shaving mirror this morning to the joy of the East End.

Rose looked openly at the chemist's right hand. 'Were you the one that got that sniper just before he got you, Mr Hawkins?'

He glanced at her keenly and smiled. 'Aye. I got him, miss.'

'Well, I never, dad! Fancy you knowing that, miss!'

Rose concentrated her attack on the old man. 'So you'll remember the Army's insistence on shaving even if the water's stone cold, there's just enough to cover the bottom of a mug and the roof's caving in. But I think the Army's right. Having a shave makes men feel better, especially wounded men.'

'I'll not say as you're wrong, miss. But a promise is a promise.'

No longer to his daughter. 'Shame, that's what it is, dad. Wicked shame. Don't like to see a poor young gentleman like that. It's not right, dad.'

'You don't have to tell me that, my girl.' He hesitated. 'If you'll pardon the liberty, miss – madam – would the gentleman be your husband?'

Rose shook her head slowly and rapidly evolved the, unborn to that moment, Plan C. Right, she thought. I don't care how low I've to hit for him – for them. She said very quietly, 'I'm afraid my husband was killed in the retreat to Dunkirk. That officer was wounded at Alamein.' She looked Mr Hawkins in the face. 'He's lost both feet, two-thirds of his left leg and his right is still in plaster with one old wound still seeping pus.'

Mr Hawkins shook his head and his daughter mopped her eyes. 'It's not right to say no, dad – it's not right! Couldn't we spare the one or two?'

'My regulars'll not like it, Mabel. But –'

'You're in the right, dad! Just have to remember there's a war on, won't they?'

Johnny restrained his joy until they had moved on. 'Four first go! Prise two out of Elderson's over the road and we beat Sister's jackpot.'

'We may do that even if we draw a blank at Eldersons. The Hawkins's dished out two wizard tip-offs. It seems that Jenks, the tobacconist's just this side of the Crown has a one-chair barber shop in his back room and –'

'Whoopee!'

'Wait for it! And the ironmonger's just beyond the Crown is run or owned or whatever by one Walt who does –'

'A nifty line in scythes?'

'Does a neat line in you ask for it he's got it. Mr Hawkins wouldn't be at all surprised if old Walt hadn't the blade or two in his stock as there's no saying what old Walt has in his stock and Mr Hawkins wouldn't like to say from whence old Walt gets his stock.'

'Rosie, you're a genius! I knew your SA and glamour would swing it. Black market, here we come!'

'Let's synchronise watches first.' She edged and stopped the carriage against the half-empty window of a woman's hairdresser to let by a young woman with an infant in a pushchair. She gazed fixedly at the corrugated waves of one wig to avoid exchanging smiles with the visibly, over-whelmingly sympathetic young mother. The shop window was only perfunctorily criss crossed with anti-blast paper and she saw clearly Johnny's reflection, friendly salute and the tightening of his face as the pushchair was trundled ahead. 'It's ten to twelve already, Johnny. Those nice dames in the Tudor Rose'll want to shove back the tables they'll shove out for us by twelve-fifteen when they start serving lunches. Shall we stop for coffee first? If time runs short, I'll come back on my bike this afternoon. Not early closing. That's Thursdays here.'

He was immediately concerned. 'I'm a selfish sod. Terribly sorry, Rosie. Of course you're panting for coffee after heaving this bloody pram. Tudor –'

'I'm not panting. My breakfast tea's still washing round my back teeth. But you love your coffee and jolly Bath bun.'

'Only when there's nothing better on offer. This is. But a hell of a bind for you. I'm hellish heavy.'

'You weigh a ton to lift but not in this, as I've told you. Stop beating your breast or I'll tip you onto the pavement as there's no muddy ditch handy,' she retorted briskly. She had nursed too many crippled men and women not to know how clearly they detected and passionately resented even the most well-intentioned placebo in this context. They can accept the truth, she thought, because they've had to. 'I'm not at all tired and my blood's up. On?'

He removed and replaced his cap at a jaunty angle. 'Don't spare the horses, James! Over to Elderson's? Bang on.' He stretched his right arm as she steered the carriage to the edge of the pavement and gently into the road. The few passers-by smiled and the sparse traffic stopped, sympathetically.

Being a weekday morning most of the traffic in the broad main street was either horse-drawn or on two wheels. The recent long spell of unseasonably warm weather had allowed the farmers and landgirls to get ahead with their winter ploughing and the neighbouring Allied camps to intensify their ceaseless training courses. The only shoppers around were young mothers with pre-school-aged children, elderly women, and the occasional very elderly man. All the young, youngish and middle-aged men of Avonly had long disappeared into the war and many of the surnames on the memorial to the Great War that stood outside the parish church had already been duplicated on the list waiting to be added to that memorial when this war ended. They saw no service uniforms during their progress down both sides of the street. The only military vehicles in sight were a US Army jeep and small carrier parked on the stone-flagged front yard of the Crown, a public house on the same side as but about fifty yards on from the Tudor Rose that served tea, coffee and 'light luncheons and refreshments'.

The church clock finished striking twelve as they recrossed the street in triumph. A few minutes later, outside Jenks the tobacconist, they were ecstatic. 'Thirteen, Rosie! Bloody marvellous! What in hell did you say to Jenks? Poor chap looked from here about to burst into tears.'

'This and that. Now for old Walt whose stock comes from whence none care to say but all suspect.'

'Attagirl!'

To avoid jarring him she had to take him very slowly over the uneven flags of the Crown's wide front yard. She longed to take them at a run, sensing his suddenly altered mood. 'What's your bet on old Walt?'

His cap was back at a guardsman's angle and his mouth set. 'Your guess's good as mine.'

She glanced at him then crouched to lock the brakes. 'Warm enough?'

'Yes, thanks, nursie. Nor do I need the gents. I have my own plumbing arrangements.'

She straightened and stood to block his view of the parked jeep and carrier. 'Thank God for that. The only gents in Avonly, or so they tell me, is up them stairs, through the public bar and out back. Break the law of the land by tapping the black market, I'm prepared to do for you. Doing myself a cruel mischief by trying to lug you up the Crown's front steps to its gents on my back, I am not.'

Johnny smiled reluctantly. 'Spoken like a true ministering angel.'

'Ministering angel my Aunt Fanny! I'm on a date. My halo comes off with my cap.'

He hitched up the peak of his cap to look at her shining black head, the exquisite texture of her creamy complexion touched with pink at the cheeks, the liveliness and sweetness in her wide eyes and the kindness in her wide, soft-lipped mouth. She looked so wonderful when she'd had enough sleep and in civvies, he thought, that he was almost thankful for the ghastly hours she worked and all the starch at night. Only almost, as he had never been in love before and even although his intelligence kept telling him he was in love with a dream, he loved that dream very dearly. He said, 'If that's your story, you stick to it. Get tapping the black market.'

'Slave driver.'

She raced into the ironmonger's cursing it and Jenks for being so near the Crown. As all his escorts, she tried to avoid this end of the street. She was suddenly alight with anger for Johnny and the thousands of other Johnnies. Was any young man asking too much of life because he wanted to be able to potter into a pub and buy himself a pint? Damn this bloody war. Damn all bloody wars that chewed young men up and spat them out as cripples or not at all. If this damned black marketeer had blades, either he handed 'em over or she'd hold the law as a gun to his head.

The 'black marketeer' was a stout, youngish man with a greasy cap, fat face, hard little eyes and limited vocabulary. 'Oh yes, miss? Up Everly, miss? Nurse, miss? Oh yes, I sees him, miss. Was he, miss? Are they, miss? Dozen suit, miss?'

She nearly kissed him. 'Yes, please! And thank you, Mr –?'

'Walt suits, miss. Ta, miss.' Morning, miss.'

She danced back to Johnny.

'Twelve! Twenty-five! Who needs Dottie Lamour with you on the road, Rosie!' He grasped her hands scattering blades over his top rug. 'Not to worry if I'm sliced to pieces. Worth it for this. Pundits'll patch me up – give the poor sods something to do. I just wish –' he broke off gripping her hands more tightly and looking longingly at the pub 'we could celebrate in style.'

'We could have the odd half-pint out here.'

'Scrub that.' He dropped her hands. 'When next I buy a girl a drink, I'm buying the drinks. In person. Period. Anyway, when've you ever walked into a pub on your own?'

A lie would be worse than useless. 'Never. Time I did.'

'Not tonight, Josephine. Thanks, all the same.'

She glanced over her shoulder at the jeep, carrier and the steps up to the combined entrance to the public and saloon bars. 'Back in a minute.'

'No you don't!' He lunged out but she was out of his reach. 'Come back, Rosie! Want the landlord to chuck you out? He doesn't allow unescorted young females.'

'Odds on he does this one.' She went up the steps and pushed open the opaque glass criss-crossed papered door as if taking the pub by storm.

That door opened into the small, empty, saloon bar. On its left was the open doorway to the public bar that whilst larger than the saloon looked crowded by the nine or ten American soldiers either leaning against the counter talking to the large, elderly landlord, or sitting on the old black oak settles on either side of the log fire in the hearth in the far wall. Every soldier had a glass in his hand, cigarette in his mouth and cap on the back of his head.

Rose stood poised in the open doorway for the moment before she was noticed, and did a quick survey of the number of men, the size and angle of the doorway, the size of the room and the strength of the aroma of American tobacco, beer and sweet-smelling logs. Then the landlord saw her and gave her an equally quick and comprehensive survey. 'Would you be looking for someone, miss?' He called politely and every other voice stopped talking and heads turned towards her.

She stayed in the doorway and looked at the soldiers as she looked at the kitchen crew from the kitchen doorway when she needed their help, before turning to the speaker. 'Not someone in particular, thank you, landlord. I work in MO 1, you'll know what I mean –' he nodded, watching her, 'and what I need from you gentlemen' she turned to the Americans 'is help.' She explained why in detail and in the great quiet that had fallen over the public bar and removed all caps from heads and cigarettes from lips. 'Lifting that carriage,' she went on, 'will be a dodgy job. It'll be heavy and even a tiny jolt'll cause him great pain, but he would like to buy a beer for himself so –'

involuntarily she held out both hands – 'if you could –'

She had no time to finish, nor, it seemed to her, to draw another breath, before a posse of GIs had rushed passed her, out and down the steps whilst a couple more and the landlord cleared away bar stools and two or three small marble-topped tables. And then the carriage was borne in on the Americans' shoulders with Johnny, his cap on the back of his head and on his thin, fragile face the shy grin of a small boy presented with his first, longed-for watch, and the carriage was set down parallel with the counter as if it, and Johnny, were made of eggshell.

Part II

December, 1943.

6

'I'm glad your set's staying on over Christmas, Weston.'
Nurse Ames closed the log book and pushed it across the
dutyroom table. 'I just hope you all survive pushing well
into your fourth month.'

'Thank you, nurse.'

It was over a week since Rose's return from nights off
and after the report she had just been given on today's
admission, Lieutenant Bevis in SW3, she had returned to
looking and sounding a machine. Not to feeling one.
Those nights off had finally provided her with the time
and privacy in which to discover her own thoughts and
the awakening of her long dormant sexual emotions. This
last perturbed her on Johnny's and her own behalf. It
seemed to her immaterial whether Johnny genuinely loved
her and that what mattered was that he thought he did,
and that that thought was too vital to his welfare for
anyone that cared for him in every sense to risk destroy-
ing. Whilst she was in MO 1 that risk would be high;
Johnny's eyes were as quick as his mind. Once she came
off nights and the escalators moved in opposite directions,
absence, time, hospital routine and the war-ingrained
habit of forgetting yesterday, living in today and hoping,
but not wholly expecting tomorrow would come, would
help Johnny to forget her. And not only Johnny, she had
thought on nights off. Joe Arden. She sensed belatedly
that he had taken a shine to her, and was disturbed by the
depth of her dread that once she moved on the shine would
fade, and of her realisation that he was so busy and senior
that whilst she was in MO 1, even had Johnny not come

into it, as he must, between etiquette and lack of time Joe Arden – and she – were in invisible straitjackets. Damn this war, she'd thought. I could go for that man in a big way. I know it now and I haven't known that about any man since my darling Stephen and no man before him. Grandfather was right. I am a chip off the old block. He always knew what he wanted and if he couldn't have it, preferred doing without to settling for second best. The only woman he ever wanted was Grannie and he had for nearly fifty years – God – what must it be like to have such glorious luck?

Nurse Ames eased back but didn't leave her chair. She was a fair, chubby young woman with a placid manner, a Martha's Silver Medal, and a husband who was the present Senior Medical Officer in Martha's, London, and the reason why a Silver Medallist was exiled to what was regarded by both main branches of her parent hospital, as the sticks. The war had forced Martha's Matron to employ married nurses, but she refused to allow married couples to work in the same branches and as the senior residents in Martha's London and Hut exchanged places every six months during their two-year appointments, Nurse Ames had staffed in MO 1 for the last fourteen months of her marriage. She was popular with the patients and staff, and especially her juniors, who were all convinced she had only missed a Gold through her habit of treating them as human, and in private, with informality.

She went on, 'Much nicer for the patients to have you staying on. Staff changes always upset them, and particularly over Christmas. We'll be pitching home for Christmas leave every man that can possibly make it, but even so, and without more admissions, we should have around eighteen bedpatients and Midget. He won't be fit for the long trip to and from Aberdeen, but luckily he seems quite happy to stay on with his pals.' Her round face clouded. 'I'm afraid none are too happy tonight, but it's something that none have had time to know Bevis. As I've just said, I'm afraid he won't last the night. God alone knows how he's still with us, or reached us. Hasn't properly surfaced once and one wouldn't expect it with that head wound. Just surface enough to keep tugging off the oxygen mask and twitching out the blood and drip needles so often and no matter what we gave him, that Mr Arden said discontinue the lot. He's written and signed that bit in Bevis's notes.' She sighed. 'He's a big, strong boy, poor chap. Heart like a sledgehammer. Nothing anyone can do for him now beyond making sure he's free of pain and – to use that wretched euphemism – comfortable. Mr Arden's left you all the morphia in hand you'll need, and as his swallowing reflexes are still working spasmodically, get as much fluid as you can in by mouth. He can only manage a few teaspoonfuls at a time, then it dribbles out. But keep it up as if it does nothing else it'll make his mouth taste better.' Rose nodded. 'We haven't left him alone. My second-year's with him now, but how you'll manage this with just two on. I'll have to leave to you. I did ask Matron to send you a night relief, but when she asked how much nursing he required, I had to say, very little. She had to turn me down. The only relief on tonight is a Benedict's second-year. She must go to Hut 9. They've three DILs to our one, plus a full ward and one of their DILs had an emergency fore-quarter [an amputation of the leg from the disarticulated hip-joint] this evening. Yes.' She answered Rose's urgent, unspoken question. 'Gangrene had set in. Mr Arden took it off. I'm afraid this hasn't been that poor man's day. First Bevis comes in as his patient, then a fore-quarter. No alternative to facing open defeat on both counts. Nothing upsets any good doctor more than being forced to acknowledge how limited is the greatest medical knowledge, experience and skill. All good orthopod surgeons – and they don't come better than J. J. – hate amputating. However, he'll survive as he's got to, but for that poor boy's sake I hope the end comes soon and peacefully.' She stood up. 'You'll want to see him first so I'll come with you and then shoo off my second-year. You'll want us out from under your feet as you've got enough on your plate tonight.' She paused. 'Williams's temperature is down but I just don't like the look of him. I did tell you?'

'Yes, nurse.' Rose's training had wholly taken over her mind. Nurse Ames normally never repeated herself and Rose had never known her nursing instincts to be wrong. 'You said you didn't think he's cooking another abscess.'

'I don't. The picture's wrong. Watch him.'

'Yes, nurse.'

They looked at each other and in silence left the dutyroom and walked through the silent East End to SW3.

Lieutenant Bevis was a gunner, and the exception to the general rule in MO 1, in being a newly wounded admission. This morning, just after 9.0, an ATS driver had driven him up to one of the anti-aircraft gun-sites on the cliffs of a Channel coast town, to make his routine inspection as Forward Observation Officer. That site had four guns and twenty ATS personnel amongst the gun-crews. Mr Bevis had just left the car and was talking to an ATS sergeant when a German tip-and-run fighter-bomber flew in fast over the sea, soared up and released a stick of bombs.

These tip-and-runs had harassed the English south-eastern seaside towns since 1940. It took only about five minutes to fly from the French coast and by flying too low over the sea to be picked up on radar, the raiders had usually dropped their bombs and gone before RAF fighter retaliation was feasible. The inhabitants of those towns and the predominantly ATS crews 'manning' the ack-ack guns ringing that coast, regarded these 'incidents', as they were called, as routine events. Some caused considerable damage; some, little. This morning's pilot had been very skilled and his bombs had destroyed four guns and a staff car, and killed outright twenty-one young women and four young men.

Mr Bevis, the sole survivor, had had a portion of the back of his head blown off, his spine severed in two places, and the back of his body and legs badly lacerated. At first, he had been thought dead, and when found still alive had been swiftly taken to the nearest, smallish, civilian hospital, and there, without being lifted from the ambulance, given a blood transfusion and glucose-saline drip infusion

106

and, with both *in situ*, driven straight on to Everly Place.

MO 1 had not known which telephone call between 9.0 and 10.0 had announced a DIL was coming in, but within minutes of that call MO 1 knew one was due in SW3. The morning was grey and sleeting, so no beds were outside and from the shelter of open newspapers, magazines and books, MO 1 had watched the speedy removal of the black-iron bed from SW3 and its replacement by a white hospital bed on loan from the General Surgical Unit. And then, in quick, orderly procession had trundled by, an oxygen and a carbon dioxide cylinder clamped into individual, black iron, low-wheeled stands, the large glass flow-meter that would be fitted into the oxygen apparatus and the high wooden stool to hold the meter; the tall, white metal blood and drip stand; the pairs of wooden bed-blocks in rising heights; the assortment of pre-made, open spinal plaster casts in varying sizes of the largest fitting; the sterile-towel shrouded glass dressing trolleys that held the emergency dressings' setting, the emergency hypodermic tray that included long heart needles, small rubber-capped bottles of adrenalin and insulin, and glass ampules of coramine and morphine, and the emergency blood transfusion setting in a sterilized drum that was accompanied by a newly set 'cut-down' setting that would be needed if the veins were too collapsed for the insertion of a needle and the surgeons had to cut down to expose a deeper vein, or veins.

MO 1 had watched, exchanged glances, tried to force the attention back to 'Jane' in the *Daily Mirror*, *The Times's* crossword, *Men Only*, *Lilliput*, Evelyn Waugh, Edgar Wallace, Gibbon, and waited. Then, at just before 11.0, the military ambulance had drawn up outside and Sister and Nurse Ames, their faces masked and sleeves rolled above their elbows had gone out into the sleet to take and hold aloft the vacolitre of whole blood and the bottle of the drip infusion. From then on, one of the day nurses had been permanently behind the open red screen across SW3's doorway and another, and this time human and non-stop procession, had come and gone through the East End.

Sister and Nurse Ames; J. J., Old Bill, little Lomax

looking a dirty shade of green, the Resident Anaesthetist, a couple of chaps Johnny identified as the Medical and General Surgical registrars; then – black sign – the C of E padre. No relatives. . . why in hell not?. . . Live too far off? . . . Hold it! Charlie Chalmers's got the gen from the Brig via Sister. . . next-of-kin's a married sister that's just had a baby in Wales. . . parents, kid brother and sister evacuated to the States in '39. . . yes, left Bevis and his elder sister to finish off in boarding schools. . . no wife. . . twenty-two. . . tough . . . bloody tough. . . How many girls bought it? Oh Christ . . . bloody hell. . . and the AT driver. . . bloody hell. . . who the hell's got a fag?. . . thanks. . . .

MO 1 now watched the two nurses disappear into SW3 and reappear a few minutes later with the second-year, then Rose's return alone. A minute or so later she reappeared, washed her hands at one of the sinks on either side of the small wards then streaked through the East End at the top walking speed it had taken her, as most nurses, three student years to acquire. At that speed she didn't rustle starch, she crackled starch.

'Dutyroom or kitchen, Johnny?'

Johnny frowned into his carefully angled shaving mirror. 'Kitchen. She's putting Sweet Sue on as his special.'

Sam Eccles looked over his reading glasses. 'VADs don't special-nurse.'

'Snow White's an odd bod,' retorted Johnny drily. 'Only got two hands. Why's no one got round to training an octopus as a nurse? Make a bloody useful nurse, an octopus would.' He reached into his locker for his sketching block and pencils to draw an octopus in a nurse's cap, but first wrote in capitals the title of the sketch that had flashed into his mind. He wrote ENGLAND EXPECTS and then added a line of dots with such force that he dented the thick block half-through.

Rose, on one foot in the kitchen doorway, thought passionately, he's not dying alone tonight. She said calmly, to Major Fraser, Captain Flynn and Midget, 'Gentlemen, can you be angels and manage drinks alone? I have to take away Nurse Kirby.'

Five seconds later Johnny was adorning the suckerless body of his octopus with a Martha's cap, both nurses were in SW3 and Sue Kirby's blue eyes were wide with fear. 'Me? Special – him?' she muttered unsteadily.

The red-shaded lamp was on the bedtable that, as the dressing trolleys, was lined against the red-padded walls to leave clear the sides of the tilted bed that had its foot castors locked in six-inch high wooden blocks. The large oxygen and smaller carbon dioxide stands stood at either side and a little back from the bedhead with their green rubber tubes and masks looped round the headless necks, gauges registering two-thirds full and OFF. And in the pink-tinged whiteness of the bed was what looked to Sue Kirby's frightened eyes a white-turbaned young giant with faintly blurred features and dark purple patches under his closed eyes, lying stiffly outstretched in the open spinal plaster case. 'His – his face isn't cut?'

'No. Obviously, instinctively, he flung himself face down on the turf. Took it all in the back.' They stood at the foot of the bed, watching Bevis as they talked. 'They had him on his face when he first came in, but he couldn't bear that or being on his sides and seemed – seems – more comfortable on his back, so whilst he is, this is how we'll leave him.' Rose moved to one side of the bed and dropping one hand on the strong-boned, muscular, limp, right pulse checked the radial beat for a full minute on her watch. The beat was slow, but steady as the shallow respirations. A strong heart, strong lungs and a strong boy, she thought, fighting off her mingled anger and sadness at what the war had done this morning to another boy in a man's uniform and those girls in ATS uniforms – God, she mustn't think of them now, nor of their families tonight, nor that some of those girls could have been as pretty and young as Kirby or even younger.

She pulled down her mask and bending over him, in turn gently raised his eyelids. If there was anything there, a masked face would frighten him. His eyes were badly bloodshot, the pupils pin-pointed and he stared up unseeingly, and yet there was a hint of anxiety in his stare

109

that she had glimpsed when she returned to look at him alone. Still there, she thought in distress and thinking hard. With that devastating head wound that must, inevitably, be fatal, theoretically it was near-inconceivable that any part of his mind was still functioning and as certain that his restlessness had been caused purely by his reflex reactions. Only in practice, they didn't always follow the textbooks. She remembered a boy of 18 in Martha's, London, an air-raid victim, who had lived on for forty-eight hours with half his head sliced off and despite being packed with drugs, screamed for most of those hours, unless the day staff nurse was with him. Somehow, she had got through to him and given him comfort, but whether by her voice, touch or presence, no one had been able to explain. She remembered other patients, but that boy in London had been the worst head wound she'd seen, and she had to suppress her wince at the memory.

She took Bevis's right hand in both her own, and gently stroking the knuckles said quietly, clearly, 'Mr Bevis, I'm Nurse Weston, one of your night nurses and with me is another whose name is Nurse Kirby and she is going to stay with you. I'm just going to talk to Nurse Kirby for a minute or two, then you'll feel her holding your hand. All right, Mr Bevis?' She paused but neither expected nor had any response. She laid down his hand carefully and backed to the foot of the bed. 'You'll manage, Kirby,' she murmured. 'Now, listen.' Briefly, succinctly, she outlined the medical report and treatment. Then she said, 'if you're worried about anything, anytime, call me. Don't come. Call quietly.' She jerked back her head. 'They'll be listening and do the rest. Got that?'

'Yes, nurse.' Sue licked her dry lips. 'So he doesn't need oxygen?'

'Not pro tem. Not cyanosed – blue. See his lips? Pink. Not bubbly.'

Sue stiffened. 'Bubbly?'

'Rattling.' Rose ran a forefinger up and down her own sternum. 'When the lungs get congested you hear the

110

mucus rattling. If he does rattle, call me, stat . . .'

Oh no, thought Sue, oh no! I've always heard that they rattle before they – but I've never heard – oh no! She muttered, 'Yes, nurse.'

'Right. Now, a bit more. Keep your mask down.' Rose explained why. 'And don't forget this next bit; if he gets restless, call me, and even if he tries to pull off his cranial bandages don't try and hold his hands down. Don't try that ever on him or any other comatosed patient. They're often very strong – and some of his reflexes are still strong. It's a reflex action for anyone in coma feeling someone trying to hold him or her down, to struggle and sometimes hit out. This applies particularly to a strong man, but if he can somehow sense that whoever is with him is a woman his instincts will know she's bound to be weaker than he is and if she handles him gently she can soothe him where a strong man in her place might not just fail but cause a disastrously violent reaction. All the same, even if you're gentle as a feather, he may suddenly tug off that turban without warning. Won't be your fault if he does, but if he does –' she looked into the very pretty, scared face 'don't look at the back of his head. Call me whatever I'm doing, whoever I'm with, but don't look at the back of his head. That clear? It'd better be,' she was curt 'as I'm not going to have time to pick you off the floor tonight. Clear?'

'Y – Yes, nurse.'

'Good. I'll be in and out and deal with his sips of glucose-lemonade and pulse and the rest. You've just got to sit and hold his hand and talk to him.'

'T – Talk?'

Rose nodded unemotionally. 'Small talk. Not all the time. Now and then. But each time use his name and tell him yours. If anything can get through he may recognise his own name and that may – only may – help him feel that though he doesn't know where he is, whoever's with him knows who he is. Again he may – just – associate your name with your voice, but even if he can't the sound of a human voice and feel of a human hand, can comfort him.' She paused a moment. 'Wouldn't it comfort you?'

Sue nodded and stared at the outstretched figure that looked to her as still as death, as she had never seen death. She had worked in wards where patients had died, but her position as a junior amateur amongst professional nurses and the screens round the DIL beds had sheltered her from the sight of the dying and the dead. Had she been a VAD in a service hospital she would have been unlikely to have been so sheltered, but in Everly Place the VADs were treated as junior probationers, and, officially, not allowed to nurse DILs or to assist in Last Offices – i.e. the immediate closing of the eyes, raising of the jaw and straightening of the limbs after death, and then, one hour later, the washing of the whole body and the packing of all wounds and bodily orifices performed by the senior ward nurse.

'I'll wait whilst you get a chair for yourself from the dutyroom, and then you're to stay put in here unless I –' Rose tapped her bib 'call you out. You'll be all right and don't get het up about what you don't know, as you can't be expected to know what you haven't been taught or done before. I'll have to get you out for turning the others, but I'll cope with the ward and you'll cope in here. I'll be in and out.' Rose paused again, and the sudden strength beneath the youthful curves of her face astonished her junior. 'Over my dead body' breathed Rose 'is he going alone tonight. No family, no friends. Just us. Get me?'

'Yes, Oh yes.' Sue fled for her chair. She had just vanished down the hall passasge when the hall curtains were thrust aside and Sam Eccles, whose position in 18 gave him the best East End view of those curtains, hissed, 'C of E padre, Nurse Weston.'

Everly Place lay in the parish of St Margaret's, Avonly, the church by the Great War memorial and from peacetime its vicar, Mr Stamford, had combined the work of hospital chaplain with his other duties. Mr Stamford was in his late sixties, sturdy and white-haired and his habit of never appearing in the hospital without his cassock frequently confused new patients into addressing him as 'Father'. Mr Stamford privately approved of this. He was a mild man with leanings as High as his parochial church council would permit; his sermons were long and soporific, but his parishioners agreed the old vicar meant kindly even if he did carry on and on. On his many, regular ward visits, he often had occasion to compliment the ward sisters on how many of their patients were enjoying restful naps, and usually, at his appearance in the hall, the East End closed its eyes and the West braced itself manfully. Mr Stamford seldom visited the hospital at night, as his age, the lack of petrol, and elderly bicycle that was his main means of transport, forced him to acknowledge the wisdom in his wife's reminder that the hospital had quite enough work to do without his adding to it. Mrs Stamford had not protested tonight, though the day's sleet was turning to snow. She had lost both her brothers in the Great War and last year their only son had been killed near Benghazi. 'Ride carefully, Gervase,' was all she said wrapping a second scarf round his neck. The cassock's skirt on the bicycle worried her greatly, but she had been married to her husband for forty-one years.

Rose helped him divest himself of his tweed cap, two long scarves, and the old Army greatcoat he had worn in France as a military chaplain. 'Thank you, nurse, my dear, thank you. How is that sad young Bevis?' he asked anxiously in what he intended as a murmur and in his resonant voice echoed around like a stage-whisper.

'No change, I'm afraid, Mr Stamford.' She shook the greatcoat free of melting snow, draped it over two spare oxygen cylinders and covertly watched Sue Kirby disappearing into SW3 with a chair. The East End made no pretence of sleep and every head but Johnny's swung like a Wimbledon crowd. Johnny's guarded eyes slid from side to side and then stared at the completed octopus on his block. He thought a moment then drew an outsize pocket torch in the first of the eight suckers.

Mr Stamford replaced his dried, steel-rimmed spectacles and peered at Rose, 'I know you, nurse! Don't tell me – I have it – Nurse Weston! But, where – ?'

'Hut 9, July to September on days.'

'Indeed, it was! You were the nurse that played most beautifully for my ward services – such a blessed talent and much appreciated by the men, I assure you, but doubtless you have little time for exercising your musical gift on night duty?' But what else was it? Ah! He had it! It was after one of the visits dear Dorothy had paid Hut 9 that she had rummaged in the attic for an old copy of *The Tatler* and showed him this girl's wedding photograph – charming bride – poor child – but yes, indeed most gifted – only grandchild – dear Dorothy never forgot a face even if she had only seen it in newspapers. Dear Dorothy would be most interested when he returned home, but that must await and he must collect his thoughts. 'May I see him?'

'Of course, Mr Stamford. Please.'

She took him through the East End feeling split between her gratitude to him for coming out at night in this weather at his age and his effect on her conscious patients. The sight of any padre at night had them hearing the silent sounding of the Last Post. They were smiling with their lips and chorusing 'Good evening, sir,' like over-polite schoolboys. Only Johnny didn't look up and was concentrating ostensibly on the outsize thermometer he was attaching to the second sucker. She glanced at his lowered head then back to see all was well in the West End and caught Major Chalmers's eye. He held up a hand, she raised one in reply, and having shown Mr Stamford into SW3, streaked back. 'Yes, major?'

He beckoned her closer. 'Peter Williams'll shoot me down if he hears this, nurse, but you'll want the gen. Starting the shakes – only these last few minutes – teeth going like castanets – sorry to bother you, but –'

'Quite right and thanks.' She streaked on to SW1.

Major Williams was 39, a former Oxford don, who had volunteered for the Army in the winter of '39, enlisted as a trooper in a county yeomanry and gained his majority last year. In the final advance in Tunisia this May the bones of his right leg had been shattered and the leg itself all but shot off. He was a slightly built black-haired man with a

114

dark-eyed, sallow, aesthetic face that Goya might have painted and with great powers of resilience. In MO 1 he had already overcome pneumonia, general septicaemia, and the series of deep-seated abscesses that for months had kept his temperature swinging and a yellow SIL label on his bed-ticket. But for the last couple of weeks his temperature had settled, his tissue wounds had begun to show clear signs of healing, the plates Joe Arden had used to pin together the shattered femur, tibia and fibula had even more clearly taken with a good union, and Sister had confided to Nurse Ames her hope that he would be off the SIL and in the main body of the West End before Christmas.

When Rose reached his bedside his eyes were closed, his lips clamped together to control his chattering teeth, his hands gripped his arms clamped across his chest under the top bed-clothes for warmth and to lessen the uncontroll-able shivers that were already making his white bed tremble despite the steadying weight of his large iron bedcradle and the fracture boards beneath his mattress. The foot of his bed was raised on four-inch blocks purely to prevent his ten-dency to slip down the bed and keep him in the semi-seated position that was essential for all long-term bedpatients to counteract the constant risk of hypostatic pneumonia, and owing to his medical history, especially in his case.

After her quick, appraising glance, Rose immediately lifted the footrail, kicked aside the blocks and gently lowered the foot of the bed to the floor. Feeling the move-ment, he blinked painfully, 'J – J – Just th – the – sh – shakes –'

'I know, major. Blankets coming.' She streaked off think-ing, I know he's starting a rigor and though I'm not yet sure what's causing it, from the violence of its start in a few minutes his bed's going to be shaking the floor. She grabbed an armload of clean blankets from the linen-room and four empty rubber hot water bottles and on her return ducked into the kitchen and dumped the bottles on the table. Midget was at the sink, Major Fraser heating milk. 'Could you –'

'We will!'

'Thanks.' She shot on and covered Major Williams with six doubled blankets. Her hand was on his wrist under the covers when Major Fraser came in with the four filled bottles under his one arm. He wore a navy silk dressing gown with the empty sleeve neatly pinned in the breast pocket and cream pyjamas and now looked his real age. He waited till she had the bottles in place. 'Door screened, nurse?' he asked softly.

'Can you?'

'Of course. Anything else?'

'Could you wait outside?'

He nodded and vanished. When she next looked round, the red screen was up.

She was still taking Major Williams's pulse and studying him clinically. The chattering and shivering were increasing and his face was taut, yellowish and reminded her of the faces of two men in Hut 9. This could have a septic focus, she thought, but I don't think so. Ames was right. The picture's wrong, but I've seen this picture, even though there's nothing in his old notes about it. She said quietly, 'Please don't try and talk as you could bite your tongue. Just blink if the answer's "yes". Crashing headache?' He blinked. 'Queasy?' Another blink. 'Enough to want to be sick?' No blink. 'Any new pain or just ache in that right leg?' No blink. 'Ever felt just like this before?' Rapid blinks. 'In hospital?' No blink. 'Just one more then I must get more blankets. In Africa did you ever have a bout of malaria and not report it?' His eyes squinted open, painfully, apologetically and having nursed him for so long she knew what he was trying to tell her. 'I know. No MO handy so you swallowed extra bags of mepracrine and sweated it out.' She patted his cold hand gently. 'You and half the British Army. Not to worry. Back at the double.' His cold, shaking hand gripped hers in thanks. She gave it a little squeeze and backed away.

The West End exchanged glances as she raced by. 'Roller skates, nurses for the use of in order, eh. Sandy?' observed Major Chalmers to Major Fraser sitting on the side of his own bed. Major Fraser nodded sombrely and at

116

the opposite end of the divided ward Johnny completed the giant hot water bottle slung from the fourth sucker – the third held a bedpan – and started loading the fifth with a stack of blankets.

Rose laid the tenth blanket over Major Williams and lightly rested one hand on his forehead. Temp. still dropping subnormal, she thought, and if I could take it, it probably wouldn't register on our thermometers and I daren't use one orally or rectally as the way he's shaking he'll snap the glass. If I'm right, this 'cold stage' will last about another hour and then his temp.'ll rise and at the peak of the 'hot stage' it could hit 106 or over and push him into delirium and then coma and – no! If it shoots higher I'll bring it down with a tepid or really cold sponge, but I'll bring it down. He's not gone through all he has for that! I'm damned if he is and if this is a recurrent bout of malaria I know how to deal with it and deal with it, I will. She said gently, 'You'll warm up fairly soon, major, and after the sweats you'll have a good sleep.'

'Th – th – thank –'

'Please.' She touched his lips lightly. 'Don't talk. Back in a minute.'

Major Fraser rose from his bed as she came round the screen. 'What, nurse?'

'Could you watch for the padre and ask Midget to make him a small pot of tea, please? I can't let him go home without a hot drink, but I haven't time to entertain him. Could you? In the dutyroom.'

'No trouble, nurse. Anything else?'

'Just a general watch as I've got to 'phone. Bless you – all.' She raced on to the dutyroom.

'Mr Lomax for Male Orthopaedic 1. Emergency, switchboard.'

'Not another. You'll be lucky, nurse. Mr Lomax's doing a cut-down with Mr Hodges in Hut 9 –'

'Then get me Hut 9, please,' snapped Rose, seething with impatience over the hospital rule that insisted the houseman be immediately informed when a patient in any of his wards started a rigor. Damned waste of time, she seethed, as there's nothing any doctor can do at this stage as the only treatment is nursing, but if I don't let that clot know stat., Night Sister and Sister MO I'll take me apart.'

'Hut 9. Nurse Franklin, speaking.'

Hell. The junior. 'Nurse Weston from MO 1. Mr Lomax, please. Emergency.'

'I'm awfully sorry, Nurse Weston, but Mr Lomax is scrubbed-up and assisting Mr Hodges with – oh – could you hold on, please –' she covered the mouthpiece and Rose heard her talking to someone her end but not what she said.

'Arden, here, Nurse Weston. What's the emergency in MO 1?' He could have been asking for a weather forecast.

She was too worried and impatient to have time for personal emotions or to obey the strict, traditional rule that forbade nurses to diagnose. She told him the truth as she saw it.

'You're very probably right, nurse. Most things most commonly look like what they are. Mr Hodges is on tonight, but as he's tied-up I'll let him know the situation then come on over. Bevis?'

'No change up to a few minutes ago.'

'Thank you, nurse.' He rang off.

She slammed down the receiver and shot back to SW 1 as Mr Stamford came slowly from SW3, Major Fraser advanced towards him, and Johnny, having attached a surgical dressing trolley to the sixth and a vacolitre of blood to the seventh, added to the eighth sucker a huge mug labelled COCOA.

7

Sue Kirby re-seated herself on the edge of the chair and even although again upon her own, surreptitiously dried her palms on the dress skirt under her apron like a guilty child concealing sticky fingers. She listened longingly to the murmur of voices beyond the screen, to Major Fraser telling Mr Stamford there was tea waiting and to Mr Stamford saying he couldn't deny a hot cup would be most welcome. She guessed Weston had had to ask the major to cope – he was marvellous about coping – they were all marvellous – especially when there was a flap on.

Flap both ends tonight, she mused unhappily, giving her palms an unnecessary extra rub. Poor Weston. Bad enough having to cope with senior and junior routine without flaps. The crew would deal with drinks, but she'd have all the four-hourly medicines, TPRs, dressings, and all the bedpatients 'backs' before she settled them all round on her own. ('Backs' was the composite term for the massaging with methylated spirits then dusting with talcum powder of the buttocks, elbows, ankles, and where exposed, shoulder-blades done thrice-daily by the day staff, and night and morning by the night, to prevent bedsores. The appearance of any bedsore was a major nursing crime that had to be reported to Matron and resulted in the ward sister and night senior being severely reprimanded and a record of this entered in their personal hospital files.)

The East End were still murmuring about Major Williams. Mr Player was saying something about 5 to 1, malaria, 10 to 1, another abscess. Captain Eccles was sure it was malaria. 'Midget says old Sandy says he's now yellow as a Jap deserter and his bed's bouncing all over the shop. Sounds like typical malaria shakes, if you ask me.'

She longed to ask him and for much more. She couldn't understand how Major Williams could suddenly have malaria when he couldn't have been bitten by the right sort of mosquito for ages and ages. She didn't dare nip round the screen to ask and wasn't tall enough to peep over it even on her toes. Anyway, Weston said she must stay put and this staying put was so awful that she wished Mr Stamford hadn't gone even although the sight of him creaking onto his knees had frightened her so much more that when he'd asked her to join in the Our Father she hadn't at first been able to remember the words she had known since before she could read. She had been relieved he'd prayed with his eyes shut and hadn't seen her hesitation or kind of shudder when they said '. . . Thy will be done . . .'

Stop thinking about that as you never understand things like that, she scolded herself, and hold – his – hand.

She forced herself to do so and to watch the closed face under the white turban with the deepening purple bruises beneath the eyes. Weston had explained, but she, Sue, still didn't follow why a blow on the back of the head should give him two black eyes. Nor why she could still feel the slow thump of his pulse when he was dying. Not that Weston had actually said 'dying'. Proper nurses never did. They said 'very poorly', or 'I'm afraid, not too well' when 'dying' was what they meant. And she'd said talk. Small talk.

She cleared her throat nervously and whispered, 'I hope you're comfortable, Mr Bevis. I'm sitting with you. I hope you're warm enough –' she said keep using names 'Mr. Bevis. I'm Nurse Kirby, Mr Bevis and – um – I'm the night VAD, Mr Bevis – that means I'm the night junior and – and my name's Nurse Kirby, and it's me that's holding your hand, Mr Bevis . . .'

Was she talking too much? Not enough? What did it matter when it was like talking to a log – NO! She mustn't think of him like that. She must, MUST, think of him like Mr Player, Captain Eccles, Mr Duncan and all the others – after all, only this morning when he got up he must've been – NO! Don't remember that . . . Thy will be done . . . no, it wasn't – it wasn't – it couldn't be – she didn't have to understand, she just knew!

How could she know? She wasn't clever. She hadn't even passed School Cert. but Mummy and Daddy hadn't minded and Michael said he was bucked as hell she hadn't. 'Who needs brains with your face, darling? Who wants a brainy wife? Not this bloke.' But Michael was awfully clever – though he'd be livid if she told him so – and it was because of something he'd once said that she knew this wasn't God's will. 'God doesn't pilot the bloody aircraft or drop the bloody bombs, darling. Our job. Ours, and Jerry's. So we do it, bloody fools that we are as only owls and bloody fools fly at night. Not that night ops. are as dodgy as the day, as the poor bloody Yanks' losses prove.'

What about the ghastly RAF night bomber losses? What about – oh, baby! Michael hadn't rung this evening so his station must be pre-operational and in about an hour C for Charlie would be taking off – oh, no – oh no – only four more – but – FOUR – no, mustn't think – only how could she stop thinking? When she knew that in a few hours' time C for Charlie's bombs would do to some people what that Jerry's bombs had done this morning to – him – and all those girls and men – all those poor, poor ATS girls . . .

She screwed shut her eyes to try and shut out her first mature insight into the fact that the basic purpose of war was to kill. She didn't know how long it was before a slight movement made her jerk open her eyes and she was half out of her chair before she realised who had come in quietly on his own. 'I – I wasn't asleep, Mr Arden.'

'I saw that, nurse. Please don't get up.'

She obeyed and watched apprehensively as he walked to the other side of the bed to take Mr Bevis's pulse and look into his staring, unseeing eyes. She supposed Mr

Arden must be acting registrar tonight, but wasn't sure, as she never had any direct contact with the doctors and was now so perpetually tired on nights that she couldn't remember things she didn't have to, like whose turn it had been to act registrar last night. But the grey suit under his white coat reminded her that he was a pundit. Pundits had to be escorted. Weston couldn't know he was here. Should she call her? Or ask him, first?

Joe glanced at her and said quietly, 'Nurse Weston knows I'm here, nurse.'

She was so relieved he'd spared her that decision that she smiled shyly, 'Thank you, Mr Arden.'

He nodded pleasantly, stepped a little back and stood looking down at the bed. She watched him with more interest than apprehension. He stood with his wide shoulders hunched, hands in his pockets and head lowered and she had noticed that that was how doctors always stood by patients' beds. Only he didn't look to her now like all those other doctors that had always looked to her as if they were thinking clever, important thoughts and knew exactly what to do even though so often it seemed to her all they actually did was stand and stare. Mr Arden looked as if he knew that really was all he could do for Mr Bevis and it upset him very much. It must, she thought, as all the proper nurses say he's awfully clever and the patients say he's awfully kind. She felt ghastly to be so helpless now and she was just a dogsbody that no one expected to know anything or do anything even a little bit important. Far more ghastly for Mr Arden – and she couldn't stand this silence. She said nervously, 'I've been talking to Mr Bevis. I don't think he heard me but Nurse Weston said I should and hold his hand.'

'Good.' He smiled at her. 'You're the person that can help him now, Nurse Kirby.' He backed out as quietly as he had come in and she looked after him in wonder. She hadn't known he had such a sweet smile and as everyone said he never wasted words and always meant what he said, he must have meant that.

Suddenly she felt less frightened and without realising

what she was doing began stroking with her left hand the back of the strong limp hand linked in her right. And then she nearly fell off her chair in the shock of the weak movement of his linked fingers. Did he want her to let go? No. He was trying to grip her. Only very weakly, but trying. As if – as if he was glad she was there. Should she call Weston? If you're worried, she'd said, but this wasn't worrying. This was the kind of thing the other patients had done when she'd held their hands for little whiles at night. Mostly that had been on Weston's nights off as the patients didn't like her relief very much as she would flap. Often at night Weston sat with them holding their hands and talking quietly when they couldn't sleep because their wounds hurt, or just ached and ached, and they were worried about their families, or lonely because they'd no families to worry about or for them. She had noticed that after sitting with them and giving them hot drinks Weston generally got them back to sleep without tablets, though she always gave them tablets before their aches turned into pains. Her relief didn't. 'Night Sister won't like it, Kirby' she flapped, as if what Night Sister liked was more important than the patients, and though, like Weston, she was an SRN and allowed to give out drugs so long as they had been written-up by the doctors. Juniors were forbidden to give out any medicines, so she'd copied Weston's other ways of soothing the patients. It had often worked and always made her feel she was really nursing and taught her much more about the patients as they then told her things about themselves she would never have heard on days. On days all she ever seemed to do was skivvy. Nothing but cleaning, cleaning, cleaning, she thought, looking down at her small, roughened hands.

She said impulsively, softly, but clearly, 'I'm sorry my hands feel like sandpaper, Mr Bevis. I've slept in gloves, used tons of vaseline, nothing works. My husband says they're worse than his beard – oh, sorry, Mr Bevis – this is me, your Nurse Kirby, Mr Bevis – still here and I'm not leaving you, Mr Bevis, dear.'

She didn't hear herself and in the East End only Joe

Arden, drying his hands at the sink just outside, Johnny and Sam Eccles overheard. And involuntarily the two last exchanged a look of mutual recognition that was one both normally avoided as carefully as they avoided referring to each other's or their own crippled bodies. In that brief shared look was an element that was close to envy of the comatosed man that would be spared from facing what they must for every remaining day of their lives that both knew could last for years. Neither wanted to die; but they wanted passionately to live as other, healthy young men and to live in the hopes that time might turn sour but their present intelligences could accept as permissible. They shared that look in silence and then looked quickly down at the sketching block and book in their respective hands.

Joe, replacing the hand towel, saw that exchange and heard the voice of their silence. He glanced with professional impassivity at Rose flitting from West End bed to bed with the 'backs' tray, then moved to Johnny's bedside. 'What the devil've you drawn, Johnny?' And after a closer inspection of the laden octopus, he smiled. 'Very apt. Done one of yourself being returned drunk and disorderly by an armoured division of the United States Army?'

Johnny's thin, lively face lit up. 'Not yet, sir. You're right. I should. That was a bloody good party.'

'So I've gathered from all sides. The initial rumour had the Yanks taking over Everly Place. Considerable come-down to discover all you'd done was corner the English black market in blades and the Yanks quota of gum and fags.'

'And caaandies, sir.' Sam Eccles lowered his book. 'Not to mention the Bourbon the Brigadier's saving for Christmas. Or shouldn't I have let out the strong drink?'

'I'm just a civvy surgeon, Sam. Not subject to military discipline. Yes. I did hear the CO of Johnny's new buddies paid an official call on the Brigadier bearing gifts. Very decent gesture.'

'Sorry, sir – as you were –' George Hall put in 'not Johnny's buddies, Johnny's Private Army. Troops report every visiting day, all bearing gifts and giving the green light to the nurses but having noble natures we forgive 'em and eat their caaandies and smoke their fags. Can't you smell 'em.'

'Now you mention it, George.' Joe strolled over to Sam Eccles as if this were a social occasion and the smell of gangrene was not so clinging to the back of his nose and throat that he had difficulty in discerning the stronger scent of American tobacco in the odiferous atmosphere. 'Incidentally, Sam, I've also heard the Yanks are keen to have you go along to their Christmas concert. Very generously they're laying on transport for all that can make it from here and the hut wards. How about it?'

'What do I say if I'm offered a slug of Bourbon, sir?'

Joe Arden's carefully casual grey eyes recognised in the pale, square face a determination that equalled his own and that increased his now constant concern for Sam Eccles' present and future. The ulcer over his coccyx was healing slowly, but well; on paper he was doing well, and his outward behaviour to the whole staff was that of a model patient. But none of us has yet really made contact with him, he thought, as he's determined to fight things out on his own and resents our help strongly and understandably.

He said casually, 'Cheers. I looks towards you. Down the hatch. Bottoms up. Take your pick.'

Sam smiled superficially. 'I'll think it over.'

'Do that.'

'That from Sam,' called Johnny, 'means "affirmative." Sam's legal mind never lets him say yes or no. Weighs every word and bungs in a bill for six shillings and eight-pence. Right, Sam?'

'Half-a-guinea if you want it on paper.' Sam picked up his book.

Johnny laughed almost naturally. 'If I don't get the Purple Heart from Ike in person for cementing Anglo-American relations I bloody should.'

'Bloody egotist!' protested George Hall. 'How about our Nursie Weston?'

'All fixed.' Johnny glanced almost naturally at Rose in

125

the West End. 'I've got her lined up for a Congressional Medal of Honour.'

And on present showing, Joe observed covertly, a slipped disc. She had climbed upon the footrail of a bed-head, leaned over the top and with both arms extended and hands gripping the sides of the red rubber undersheet and using her slender back as a lever, was hauling up the bed the mattress of a patient in a double hip spica. Joe had to control his urgent desire to rush to her assistance. Johnny was not the only highly observant youngster around, even if in this context he was infinitely the most vulnerable. Did she know the poor boy was so in love he could barely keep his eyes off her or her name out of any conversation, he wondered, waiting another minute or two before taking another look at Williams. He suspected she did, but only from his dead wife's confidences during their short very happy marriage and his sisters in their mutual adolescence. He had loved his wife beyond measure and grieved after her death in that measure; because he had known *that* great love, he recognised the new growth within him and that it was growing gently, as love does. Sexual attraction was a thunderbolt and often, just as shortlived. Love needed time and for that, for the first time since the sweet Dutch doll's face had begun haunting him, he was finally grateful. Just as well he'd had so little time to spend with her, and knew so relatively little about her, after those few minutes he had spent alone with the vicar in the dutyroom. Those minutes had been long enough to tell him all he would ever need to know about Rose Weston, he decided, with the conviction of an intelligent man in his professional and personal prime who belonged to a generation conditioned into self-control, self-denial, and the acceptance of the obligations that accompanied their privileges as men in what they accepted without question was man's world. To men so conditioned, their honour was not superficial gilt, but as essential an aspect of their daily lives as clean shirt-collars and well-shaven faces. The prospect of allowing themselves to be put in the position of even being suspected of being fortune-hunters, was unthinkable. 'I disremember the precise terms of old Sir Henry's will,' the vicar had said, 'but from the best of my recollection of my dear wife's account – she'd read it in the newspapers – that most estimable young Nurse Weston inherited not far short of two million pounds. A most considerable inheritance for any young lady – but most worthy, would you not say, Mr Arden?' Most. And as well to know it, thought Joe Arden walking slowly up the long ward and unconsciously, limping.

Major Williams had stopped shivering and regained control of his teeth, but his headache was much worse and he lay very still under the extra blankets and hot water bottles. His eyes were closed as he found unbearable even the soft rays of the red-shaded lamp on the floor. He didn't hear anyone approach his bedside or know he was being watched until he felt the gentle fingers on his wrist. 'Don't need anything thanks, nurse,' he muttered and blinked 'oh, you again, Mr Arden. Damn the anopheles.'

'A damnable insect. Head very bad?'

'Little chap with the hammer in action behind the eyes.' He sighed. 'As before.'

'I'm sorry – and to keep you talking, but can you remember when you had the last bout?'

'The last? When? Yes. Just after Wadi Akarit – early April.'

'That wasn't the first?'

'No. That was quite a nasty go – couple of weeks before Alamein. Only lasted a few days.'

'Never reported it?'

Major Williams smiled weakly. 'Bit far from an MO.'

'Just a few hundred miles of desert between you?'

'Just about. Anyway, knew the form. Seen it often enough. Swallowed mepracrine by the dozen and sweated it out. Time we'd rejoined our unit, old history. Sorry I forgot to tell you.'

'You've had other things on your mind. So this one resembles the April bout?'

'Yes. Sharp, short, that one. Just one night.'

'Good. You're beginning to warm up.'

'Hitting the highs and much sweats to come.'

'Then the good sleep. Thanks for talking. Take it easy as you can.'

'Thanks. Before you go – how's the gunner?'

'Not too well but sleeping. I hope you get some soon.'

He moved quietly away and when in the West End hesitated then went in to talk to the Brigadier. A few minutes later he walked slowly back to the hall followed by the guarded eyes of all the West End but Major Fraser. The watchers were old hospital hands, and J.J.'s limp perturbed them as much as Old Bill at his most jocular. Thumbs down signs, both.

Major Fraser had returned to sitting on the side of his bed and was lost in his own thoughts of the confidence he would only share with his wife when he wrote his daily letter to her, tomorrow. Their only daughter was 15, and at a boarding school in the north of England; and next week he would see for the first time in three years. He had talked to her on the telephone several times since his return and rejoiced at the prospect of their reunion. His wife said Jean was growing into a very bonnie lassie and there was no doubt in her mind that they were going to have a wee problem with Jean's laddies. With that problem he would be amused to deal. But a very different problem were Jean an heiress, or for Jean were she a young attractive widow and one of the most financially eligible girls in the UK with neither father nor uncles to protect her. The only child of only children, mother dead many years. She probably had a Trust that managed her affairs; nevertheless, to spread the word would be no way to repay all she had done and was doing for the chaps. Very decent chaps, but only human. He just hoped the old padre managed to recall all this before he opened his mouth too often – tonight, of course, the poor old chap had been so knocked for six over young Bevis that he'd blethered like an old woman, thought Major Fraser, and then being fairminded, corrected himself. Chaps of all ages enjoyed a gossip as much if not more than women and never more so than when the main subjects were

128

women or money. If it got around, it wouldn't be from him. He glanced at J.J. writing notes alone at the desk. Nor him, if the padre had spilled the beans. An old soldier in more ways than one; see all and say nowt.

SW1 and SW3 were unscreened when, at 5.45 a.m., Rose removed the linen shade and pushed up the flex of the desk lights and turned on the main ward lights. In the open-doored glowing red cavern Major Williams was deeply asleep in his third clean pyjama jacket and total change of bedding since just before midnight when his temperature peaked at 105° and the profuse sweating started. His temperature and pulse were now down to normal.

The door of SW3 was closed and hid the bare white hospital bedstead still smelling of the strong carbolic solution with which Rose had washed frame and spring at 3.30. On the floor was the mattress that she had had to have Sue Kirby's help to tie into a roll to await its collection for re-stoving by one of the day porters later this morning. They had rolled the mattress in silence, their masked faces white with fatigue and frozen by their thoughts. Rose waited till they were back in the hall to say, 'Go into the dutyroom, scrub up for a good five minutes, then put on a clean apron and make our tea.'

'Yes, nurse.'

In the kitchen over tea, Rose said, 'He couldn't have died more peacefully.'

'No, nurse.'

'How are you, Kirby?'

'All right, nurse.'

Rose looked at the girl's stunned face. 'Of course you're not,' she said gently, 'but no one is after watching a patient die unless made of stone and in the wrong job. You're not and you did a wonderful job tonight, but you're right to lie. At these times, one must. Have another cup.'

'I couldn't. Honestly. I'll throw up.'

'Hold it.' Rose ducked out to the hall to see all was well in both ends, ducked back to the dutyroom, took quickly from the medicine cupboard the stock bottle of sal volatile, poured a dose into a medicine glass and took it back to the kitchen. 'Sip this. Don't gulp or it'll hit like an HE. [High explosive bomb.]'

'Must I?'

'Yes. Sip it, Kirby, and –' the telephone bell made both start and turned Sue Kirby from white to grey. 'I'll get it.' Rose fled to silence the bell.

'Night Sister speaking, Nurse Weston. I've just had to call up Mr Hodges for Hut 9 so I've informed him of Lieutenant Bevis's death and he will be in to sign the death certificate at a quarter to nine. How is Major Williams? Good. Thank you, nurse.'

Rose put down with her eyes closed, breathed deeply, then rushed for another look at the men before returning to the kitchen. 'Only Night Sister.'

She jumped off the table. 'Sorry. I just thought –'

'I know.' Rose touched her shoulder lightly, 'Knock back the rest of that revolting stuff and your tea. We must start work and as Eccles is awake we'll wash him first.'

All the heavy washings – that is, those requiring two nurses – had been done when she turned on the main lights and Sue, still more grey than white and with the stunned look in her blue eyes, pushed in the heavy wooden food trolley laden with the early morning teas. And again, the telephone rang. Rose snapped authoritatively, 'I'll get it –' and ran rather than walked to the dutyroom. Now MO 1 had quietened, it was an odd time for Night Sister to ring. Dear God, please – please – not bad news for that poor kid – not now – not ever – please – please! 'Male Orthopaedic 1 Ward. Nurse Weston, speaking.'

'Hold on, Nurse Weston,' the hospital night operator sounded as tired as he felt 'got an outside trunk call for you. Personal call. You still there, Oxford?'

Rose turned icy. 'For me, switchboard?'

A different, more distant voice answered, 'Are you Nurse Rose Weston, Male Orthopaedic 1 Ward, Everly Place Hospital?'

'Yes. This is Nurse Rose Weston speaking.'

'Hold on, please. Sergeant Pilot Michael Kirby calling. You're through now, sir.'

'Sergeant Kirby?' Rose's heart seemed to turn over in relief. 'It's you?'

'Yes, Nurse Weston! I know we haven't met but a bright and fine good morning to you!' His young voice was excited and glad. 'Sorry to prang in at this hour. I asked for you not to alarm Sue but a couple of hours back I clocked up my sixty and I know she'll want to know. May I speak to her?'

'You've – but I thought you'd four – three if you did an op. last night?'

He laughed. 'Foxed her by keeping three under the hatch. Knew she'd get a bit het up near the final run – may I –'

'Yes, of course! Congratulations and if you're cut off whilst I'm getting her I'll tell her and you ring up back –' She all but flew back to the yawning, stretching ward, and called quietly in a voice vibrating with gladness, 'Nurse Kirby, your husband wants to talk to you. He's chalked up sixty.'

Sue was by the trolley in the West End. For a second or two she couldn't move or see that every patient was smiling at her or that Rose's smiling eyes were wet.

Rose urged, 'Get weaving, Kirby and if he's been cut off, this is true. I've just spoken to him.' Suddenly Sue vanished and Major Fraser was climbing out of bed. She waved him back. 'Thanks, Major, but I can deal with teas. She'll need a few minutes on her own to get her breath.' When all the teas were out she went into the dutyroom and put her arms round the weeping girl. 'Not cut off?' she asked, eventually.

'No. Oh, no! Grounded three months after his leave. He's got three weeks from tomorrow and wants me to get leave but how can I? I'm not due off nights till next week and I've had my two weeks for this year. How can I possibly get off?'

'You just must,' Rose thought fast. 'Wash your face. Got powder on you? Use mine.' She took a compact from her dress pocket. 'Here. Wash in that hand-basin and listen.

131

See Matron directly you go off this morning. She's in the Office from eight. Go straight there and don't be browbeaten by the Office Sisters. Just say you demand an immediate interview with Matron on urgent compassionate grounds. Say that and they're stumped as no Matron can refuse to see immediately one of her nurses demanding an interview on those grounds. Got that?' Sue, drying her face nodded dumbly. 'Then tell Matron the truth. The whole truth. That you were Bevis's night special. Get me?' Again, Sue nodded. 'I'll bet she'll give you nights off from tomorrow and a week's compassionate leave and . . .'

'Michael's got three and he wants –'

'And will have you along if you use your loaf. Once you get on leave, discover you're having a baby and . . .'

'Huh?'

'Go and see a doctor. Your own at home – a RAF MO – any doctor and tell him you think you're starting a baby and are feeling sick. He'll give you an extension – no one can prove just like that if you are pregnant or not and how do you know you won't begin a baby in the next ten days?'

Sue blushed. 'I don't, but we've got to be five months pregnant before we can be released from nursing –'

'That's what the law says. It doesn't say anything about what's due to a man that's flown sixty night ops, or a girl that's done the kind of work you've done all year. You and Michael rate this break and if you've got to bend the rules a bit and lead-swing a bit to get it for him, you do both! He's your husband. He needs you and he deserves you, and you, him.'

'You really think I should?'

'Do I not! And have a wonderful time!'

'Oh, yes, we will!' Sue smiled brilliantly and, briefly. 'Only –' She gestured to the ward 'what about them?'

'They'll understand and be bucked as hell for you.'

'I expect so.' She gave a long shuddering sigh. 'I just feel so awful about leaving them.'

Rose said simply, 'One always does. Hell, every time one moves wards. But we must get back to ours or Ellie'll be here before teas are cleared.' She turned to go, then swung back. 'Do thank your Michael from me, for ringing. His call's not just what you needed, but the shot in the arm MO 1 needed this morning. A shot of hope. You'll see. Soon as you get back to them.'

She was right, reflected Sue in the East End sluice almost to the minute twenty-four hours later. She tied a long red rubber apron over her white and stepped onto the duckboard by the sink to clean and restack the used washing basins, shaving bowls and mouthwash mugs. She was ahead with her routine as for some peculiar reason this morning Weston insisted early teas went in at 5.30. The patients hadn't minded, but they never minded how early teas came in as so many were generally awake and panting for it. she hadn't liked to ask Weston why they must be early as from around midnight Weston had been in the mood she privately labelled Weston's 'One step nearer, Mr Hands and I'll blow your brains out' type. She guessed this was because they'd just had their slackest night together in MO 1. She'd noticed all the proper nurses got browned off when their wards were slack and even the most bitchy turned human when they were hectic. Not that Weston was ever bitchy, she mused through her personal haze of exhaustion, joy, and sadness at leaving MO 1. Weston had been marvellous yesterday and everything she'd said had been right. Matron had been marvellous and actually thanked her for staying on another night as Ashley-Ellis wasn't due back from nights off until tonight. J.J. had been marvellous. He'd come into the kitchen alone whilst she was cutting the breakfast bread to congratulate Michael and say that MO 1 was going to miss her. She'd been so thrilled she couldn't remember what she had said to him but it must've been all right as he had just smiled his sweet smile and gone away. And Michael had been gloriously marvellous and so pleased and so was she – except about leaving – them.

They couldn't have been more marvellous, and she'd done so little for them and they needed and would go on needing, so much help, she thought, drying and restacking basins and bowls. Until she came on nights here she hadn't realised how much courage it took to stick being bedridden for months and months and how this sort of thing always happened after all battles. Awful to leave them knowing they'd still be here and others would be coming in, and some of them would be like Mr Player and Captain Eccles and have to stay here or later in military convalescent homes for ages and ages or – for always.

'Nearly done, Kirby?'

She glanced round and her eyes widened. It was only about 6.10, but Weston had changed into the clean apron she normally put on at 7.0. 'Just the mouthwash mugs, then the bottles [urinals] and tidying up, nurse.'

'Leave it and come back. The Brigadier wants to see you. Here.' Rose produced, apparently from the air, a Red Cross apron. 'I hope you don't mind my getting this out of your case. Change here and use this.' Again she handed over her powder compact. 'Got a comb? Use it. Your hair's a bit wild.'

Sue wondered wildly if Weston had gone batty. Nurses were forbidden to use sluices as changing-rooms. Anyway, she never changed her apron in the mornings until after pulling out the beds. But as Weston still looked in her 'One step nearer, Mr Hands . . .' mood, she obeyed.

'That's better. Get off to the Brig. I must finish my report.'

Sue obediently jog-trotted up the long ward feeling far too puzzled to notice more than absently that every patient was reading, none looked up, and that Midget and Captain Flynn were sitting on their beds instead of being in the kitchen. She only noticed Major Fraser was in the wrong place when he rose from the Brigadier's locker. 'Nurse Kirby reporting, sir. Shall I – ?'

'No, no, Sandy. Standby.' The Brigadier, a small, neat man with his remaining leg in traction, smiled quietly and fingered his neat grey moustache. 'Ah, Nurse Kirby! Last morning, eh? We'll miss you. And – er – as the senior officer present it is my very pleasant privilege to offer you a vote of the most sincere thanks on behalf of MO 1 and this – er – small memento.' He removed from the cover of the turn-down of his top sheet a footsquare card made from two sheets of white cardboard laced down the spine with red tape. 'Rather handsome workmanship, wouldn't you agree, nurse?'

She gazed at the card in her hands and blinked furiously. On the front was a full-length and fairly lifelike portrait of herself bearing aloft in one hand a mug labelled COCOA and in the other a saucepan labelled SCRAMBLED EGGS. The portrait was in water-colour, but surrounded by black-and-white matchstick figures on crutches, walking-sticks, in wheelchairs and spinal carriages. Every figure wore an outsize service cap to take the detailed insertion of his respective regimental badge. 'Brigadier – it's – it's all of you – and it's beautiful!'

'All present and correct , m'dear.' He tugged a few hairs from his moustache in satisfaction. 'Appropriate sentiments, within.'

She opened the card very slowly. On both insides were individual thank-you messages from every patient to which were added beneath the signatures, each man's regiment and date of arrival in MO 1. She was too moved for speech and looked with brimming eyes at the two men.

Major Fraser coughed softly, 'I think, perhaps, sir – ?'

'Just about to make the same suggestion, Sandy. Just pull m'door too a trifle – thanks, old chap. Here we are.' He pulled a large leather flask from under his bottom pillow and Major Fraser produced three sherry glasses. 'Can't have you upsettin' yourself, m'dear. Upset the chaps. Down the hatch, nurse – not a word to the good Sisters, eh?'

'Thank you, but should I? Nurse Weston –'

'Is extremely busy writing her report at the desk and it wouldn't surprise me if she has most unfortunately developed a slight cold in the head and sadly lost her sense of smell. Agreed, Sandy?'

'Absolutely, sir!'

'Your very good health, nurse, many more thanks, and

I think with this toast we should include the gallant Sergeant Pilot and Bomber Command. Sixty, eh? Very fine show. That's it. All the best.' He returned the empty glasses to Major Fraser and shook her hand. 'Take.care of yourself, Mrs Kirby, and – er – just have a word with the chaps.'

She had never drunk neat whisky before and hated the taste, but it had made her feel so different that she was able to smile and shake Major Fraser's hand as well and wish them both all the best.

She walked smiling and clutching her card, into the West End. None of them were now reading and they were all smiling and wanting to shake her hand and at the desk, Weston was smiling. Then Mr Player called 'What about us dregs?' and the whole East End started intoning 'Oh Why Are We Waiting,' and Weston suddenly moved from the desk to close almost and stand beside Major Williams's door. She looked back at Weston and – oh, baby! Weston, the most proper of proper nurses had winked at her!

The intoning stopped when she walked shyly into the East End. 'Thank you all for my lovely card – I'll keep it for always – it's lovely.' She looked around and thought, but for that foul whisky, I'd weep buckets. 'Did you draw it, Mr Player?'

'A poor thing, but mine own, nurse. Hold everything! One more small token to remember us by.' He held out a large box of American candies that had yesterday been acquired as a Top Priority from a secret source known only to all MO 1, Sister MO 1, Rose, Joe Arden, the CO, Executive Officer, several NCOs, and roughly fifty GIs in the nearest US Army camp. 'From us, to you, Nurse Kirby, and to show the nobility of our natures, we are all agreed that you may offer one – and only one – to that lucky sod, your old man, and tell him from us that we hope it bloody chokes him.'

She couldn't talk when she accepted the box, but she didn't have to, as suddenly Captain Hall, flat on his back held up and then dropped one arm. And then, softly,

136

slowly, to the tune of *Lili Marlene* and their own words, all the East End began singing to her.

They sang!

Sergeant Pilot Kirby's
Swiped our VAD,
But as he saw her first,
We guess that's got to be.
But we'll miss her cocoa –
And scrambled eggs –
And goddam toast crumbs –
In our beds,
But most we'll miss –
Our Sweet Sue,
And envy –
That sod Kirbeee.

Rose had positioned herself to watch Major Williams's sleeping face through the just-ajar door. He didn't stir at the singing and standing there, listening to the deep voices and the note of sadness that was so often present when sober men sang in unison unaccompanied, she thought how strangely typical of this war it was that the most loved war-song of all these British soldiers, and all those others she had nursed, should be this gently plaintive, lilting one they had scrounged from the enemy. Nothing martial nor flag-saving about it, so they had taken it to their hearts and for their own. Then the song ended and at the back of her mind she heard the escalators moving in different directions whilst she heard in reality . . . great meeting you . . . thanks a lot . . . see you around some-time . . . all the best . . . take care of yourself . . . cheers . . .

8

On Christmas Eve it was raining heavily when the night nurses arrived on duty together in MO 1; and as they made the expected admiring comments on the newly decorated ward, Rose was as privately shaken by the sight of the upright piano backed against the cylinders on the left of the hall passage doorway, as Jill Ashley-Ellis by the position of the tree nudging the cylinders on the right. Everly Place followed the traditional British hospitals' custom that the hospital Christmas was opened by the decorating of the wards and trees on the afternoon of Christmas Eve, and that from that evening to the morning of Boxing Day, no member of the nursing or medical staff took off duty for anything but sleep.

It was Rose's first night back from nights off which she had spent staying with the in-law cousins, a middle-aged married couple, who had rented her house in Chelsea since she had started nursing. And in the privacy of the housemaid's cupboard that doubled as nurses' outdoor uniform cloakroom she asked, 'When did the piano arrive, Corp?'

'Been here a couple of nights. Your relief said J.J. coughed it up from somewhere.' Jill was uninterested in the piano but jolly worried about that tree. 'Crazy sticking the tree there, nurse. The chaps down the outside wall can see it fine, but the chaps down the inner'll be lucky to squint the fairy on the top.'

Rose pulled off her dripping Martha's 'outdoor' hat, and mentally shelving her own curiosity thought – not much room left on that shelf. 'I'll bet the tree's just there pro tem and Sister'll want us to shift it into mid-hall in the small

138

hours when we hang their stockings. Hence the general post to get all the bedpatients nearer the hall and all the empty beds, wheelchairs, spinal carriages and spare screens to the far ends.'

'Jolly G! Haven't been on nights for Christmas before. Forgot tonight we turn F. Christmas. What fun! Do we fill their op stockings?'

'No.' Rose propped her open compact against a polish tin to fix on her cap. 'Sister and Nurse Ames'll have done them.'

Jill slapped her dripping pork-pie hat against one black-lisled calf. 'Who coughs up presents, patients for the use of?'

'You mean the ones from the ward and not their relatives? Sister's Ward Fund. She collects for it all year and gets most from the pundits. Residents and nursing staff aren't allowed to contribute.'

'I should jolly well think not!' Jill gave her damp short brown pageboy bob a perfunctory comb and skewered on her cap with long pins. 'You all get a positive pittance. Thirty quid a year or something, isn't it?'

Rose glanced at her and thought, whatever else has put him off me, it's not Grandfather's will. If the grapevine had somehow got hold if it, Jill would know. She's no green sweetie like Kirby. She hears all the inter-hospital gen and passes it on. She said, 'Forty p.a. for fourth years, thirty for thirds, twenty-five for seconds and twenty-eight for firsts as junior pros don't get super-annuation docked off.'

'I say, nurse, you're wizard at figures. Good at maths at school?'

Rose hesitated, then thought, what the hell? 'My best subject.' She changed the subject. 'Forgotten you'll need an apron?'

'Golly gosh, yes!' She rootled in her attaché case and held up a knotted handkerchief. 'Why did I do that? What did I have to tell you? Got it! Kirby hasn't come back and she's not coming. Starting a baby or something and a bit off-colour. I'm sorry she's gone – nice little thing – but

I'm jolly glad for her. The chaps'll be jolly glad. Okay to tell them?'

Rose looked at her blankly. My God, she thought, you're older than me, but I feel old enough to be your mother, only if I were, by now I'd have told you the facts of life and not left this one to me. 'They'll be glad for her, but don't rub it in.'

'Why not? Oh . . . I say.' Her large pleasant face reddened and she fumbled with her waistband to avoid looking up. 'I suppose they – they – er – miss it.'

Rose subdued her urge to retort, 'Don't we all?' by the reminder that she had been raised by Victorians and not their far more mealy-mouthed Edwardian children. 'They're normal men, Corp.'

'Suppose so.' Even her ears were scarlet. 'Somehow one doesn't sort of think that patients –' she broke off in confusion, then muttered, 'Different for men, of course – Mummy's always said so.'

I'll bet she has, and poor old Daddy, thought Rose, looking at her watch. 'Two minutes to go and Sister's on. Better get weaving. You've only got Midget.'

'You're telling me. Did I miss him last night – but worth it, as he and Johnny said the Yank concert was a positive wow and knocked spots off ENSA. I was fearfully bucked Sister managed to coax Sam Eccles into joining the party and –'

'How'd he enjoy it?'

Jill shrugged. 'You know him, nurse. Never says much. They came back positively loaded with fags and soap and the FO 1 girls said this morning when the curlers came out it looked and smelt like a beauty-parlour as the Yanks gave every female patient powder and lipstick FO 1 was thrilled.'

'The huts too from what I heard at supper.'

'Wow all round. Jolly rough only three of ours could go but the others were jolly D about being Cinderellas and fearfully bucked all the ex-PWs have got home for Christmas, except, of course –'

'Yes.' Rose cut her short. 'Sister'll be waiting. Time we jumped to it. See you, anon.'

MO 1 was down to eighteen patients with Midget the only 'up.' The reduction of the bedstate had taken place during Rose's nights off and was temporary. On the night following Sue Kirby's departure, the arrival of another convoy of wounded from Italy had refilled all the male wards in the OU. All MO 1's admissions from that convoy had been walking-wounded; none were ex-PWs; and owing to the nearness of Christmas, as soon as possible they had been fitted with new, temporary, and, where necessary, walking-plasters, then sent home to return after Christmas for further and much more prolonged treatment. The same had happened throughout the OU and every serviceman that could get home was now there; for the first time this year, every ward had a few empty beds. In MO 1, SWs 1, 3 and 4 were empty and closed; Major Williams was off the SIL and one of the three-aside bedpatients in the West End; the East End had five aside; Midget's bed was now 16, the last occupied on the right; Sam Eccles was in 15; and Johnny, directly opposite in 22, had the last occupied bed on the left. The half-open screens at the hall ends were still up but would be removed all tomorrow; and for the Christmas dinner served at lunchtime, the Brigadier's bed would be moved into the middle of the West End.

'A very depleted ward, Nurse Weston.' Sister closed the log book and remained, straight-backed, in her chair. 'You should have a quiet night, so if you and Nurse Ashley-Ellis have any artistic ideas about adding to our decorations, please put them into practice.'

'Yes, Sister.' Rose, staying seated, recognised that though the official report was over Sister had more to say, and the concern beneath the habitual sternness in her lined, beautiful face and dark eyes. Sensing Sister's uncharacteristic need for it, she prompted, 'It's a beautiful tree, Sister.'

The lace frills of Sister's cap fluttered graciously. 'Mr

Brunton's invariably are fine trees. He was in Hut 9 – before your time, nurse, years before. 1941. One of Mr Arden's patients. Tractor accident. He's a local farmer and since his discharge has every year provided all the Orthopaedic Unit's trees and with one of his carthorses and an old hay-wagon and the help of his landgirls delivered them personally to every ward. A very nice man.' She smiled quietly. 'He most kindly used the same means to transport to us Mr Arden's piano with Messrs Hodges, Arden, Thomas and Lomax and the eldest Hodges boy replacing the landgirls. The event provided my ward with much amusement.' Her smile vanished. 'I fear that, as yet, the instrument has not aroused the interest of Captain Eccles.'

Rose looked down at her hands folded in her lap. He didn't say it was his own piano, she thought. She said, 'He may feel up to trying it tomorrow, Sister.'

'Possibly, nurse. We can but hope so.'

The long promised orthopaedic registrar had still not arrived. On Rose's last night on duty, Joe had again been acting registrar. He had come into MO 1 at about 11.30 and in his anxiety for Sam Eccles, for the first time since he learnt of Rose's inheritance, he had overruled his new decision to avoid her whenever possible and when that was professionally impossible, to keep their encounters brief and strictly formal. In this context the arrival of the December convoy and proximity of Christmas were his allies, as he was exceedingly busy, and he badly needed the allies, as his heart reminded his head whenever he looked at her. He had been alone for a long time, and by God, he thought as they sat at the desk, whenever he set foot in MO 1 at night, he knew it.

'Something's got to be done about that chap, nurse.' He gazed into the darkness of the East End and mentally saw Sam's pale, square, guarded face. 'Far too quiescent. Out of character, that. He's got too much for it, but also too much to let the chinks show.'

'Yes. He's too good a patient.'

'Too bloody good. Nothing to say for himself but feeling fine, thanks, bloody good book. His love of reading is all to the good, but he can't spend the rest of his life in books. Somehow, we've got to get and keep him out of that bed, but now winter's hitting hard, going outside's written off and his unspoken but patent resentment of a wheelchair has me feeling a sadist for insisting he spends at least three hours daily in one. Ideally, he should be up in one all day.' He paused, frowning. 'Wish to God we could get Johnny into a chair. He'd have Sam running races up and down the East End. Not a chance of that for Johnny yet, I'm afraid. Not whilst there's still a hope of saving what's left of his right leg.'

She had become as careful to avoid looking at him, but at that she glanced at his profile. 'Still only a hope?'

His face was expressionless as his tone. 'In my opinion. You disagree?'

She mirrored him on both counts. 'No, Mr Arden. I'm sorry I asked that. Just wishful thinking.'

'Understandably so. But whatever the outcome there, Johnny'll bounce back as he'll fight back to his last breath. Sam's a fighter but the spark's gone out. It's got to be relit. And in my view to take the obvious course and shout for a psychiatrist would be disastrous. He's far too intelligent not to see through that and resent it and us, even more. I have suggested to him a transfer to Garden East, but he was against that. "Quite happy in MO 1, thanks, sir." ' He hesitated and nearly looked at her. 'Would you diagnose him as MO 1-itis?'

'No, Mr Arden.' She winced involuntarily and added icily, 'Just paraplegia-itis.'

'Demonstrably,' he snapped, in pain for Sam and her.

She glanced at him again. She had noticed his attitude towards her seemed to have undergone a radical change from around the time Kirby left, but, as ever, had had to postpone thinking over why this should be and whether in reality it hurt more than her pride, until her next nights off. That particular night was her eighty-fourth in MO 1. Hell of a time, she thought, and tried to remember for how much of that time she had known by heart every line of his face and found it so attractive that it was impossible to believe she had once thought him uninteresting and the same age as Old Bill. He's not just attractive and clever, she thought, but sweet and kind – and broadcasts both when he smiles. And it's not just my pride that's hurt – lay off that, Rosie! He cares like hell about poor Sam and so do I, so stop thinking and think! She thought for a few moments. 'It's a pity MO 1 hasn't a piano.'

He turned to her involuntarily and having done so couldn't turn away. 'Why?'

She looked quickly at the shadowy wheelchairs. 'He usually sleeps well, but a couple of nights ago he woke at about three and couldn't get off again for sometime. The rest were flat out, so I was able to sit and have a long chat with him. It was the longest we've ever had and apart from the night he came in, the only time he's talked to me about himself. It wasn't me that worked the trick, it was the effect of the small hours. He began talking about his school and how he used to infuriate the music master by jazzing it up when he should have been practising scales and things. He said even as a kid he loathed classical stuff and was nuts on jazz, blues, swing espcially Dixieland – you know?'

'Yes.' He sounded as if his understanding of that term was based purely on general knowledge. He had propped his elbows on the desk and was resting his chin on his locked hands. His hands were well-shaped, long-fingered and very strong, clean, habitually scented by the carbolic soap used in all the theatre and ward sinks.

Rose, glancing at his hands to avoid his face, surprised herself by asking intuitively, 'You play?'

'Occasionally,' was all he was prepared to admit. All his life music had been his great love and solace. For years in his boyhood he had cherished secret hopes of being a professional pianist. Those hopes had been demolished by the combination of the last war and the facts that his father couldn't have afforded to give him the essential musical education, and his own ruthless self-honesty that had forced him to recognise his talent as that of a first-class amateur, but at the best, second-class professional. 'Go on with what you were saying, nurse.'

'Yes. Sorry,' she apologised, having as intuitively recognised she had unwittingly strayed onto forbidden territory and shelving the insight as an additional item for closer inspection on her nights off. 'Well, I asked if he'd played in the Army at camp concerts, in the Naafi, places like that. He said yes, anywhere with a piano and all the free beer kept down his mess bills. I said did his unit call him Carrol Gibbons.' She smiled slightly and sadly. 'He said more their ersatz Fats Waller.'

Knowing he was being mesmerised by her sweet, so tired face, he forced his gaze back to the East End. They all sounded and looked asleep, he noted, but Johnny was lying with his face turned from the hall and towards the shaving mirror on his locker-top that Joe suspected was precisely angled to reflect the desk.

Rose went on, 'I've a hunch this was his big safety-valve. I could be wrong, but as I don't think I am, I wish this ward had a piano. He couldn't manage the pedals but that shouldn't matter too much if he's honky-tonking. And it would give him something to do that he really likes doing, particularly pro tem, whilst there's no one too ill for the noise. Snag is, the only three pianos in Everly Place are in hut wards that treasure and need them. The Red Cross or WVS just might be able to scrounge us one from somewhere, but that'll take time. Could well be that before they get one to us we've filled up with DILs or SILs. But if we had one over Christmas it could be a booster for him and the others.'

'Yes. A piano can provide a temporary escape.' He glanced at his hands then up and down the long ward. 'Anything of that nature'll come in handy over Christmas. This'll be the second in hospital for most of these chaps and their fifth away from home for them all. That this bunch all know each other so well is an advantage in one way, but not in another. New faces aren't automatically a tonic, but at their worst, they can provide useful counterirritants. Not that we're likely to have another convoy in this side of Christmas, as dirty weather in the Med., the Bay of Biscay, and the Atlantic is either holding up or slowing to a crawl all homeward bound hospital ships.'

She glanced at him sideways without moving her head, but their mental accord was so close that he knew it. 'Many on the way home?'

He nodded at the black shadows that were the hall curtains. 'The papers and BBC may have the Italian campaign going as planned, but from the Brig. and others I gather it's being one bloody shambles after another. Jerry's putting up a hell of a fight.'

'They all say he's a fighting man.'

'He always was.' He paused. He'd had to remind himself of his age, but not to enjoy it. Then, 'Tough on those chaps having Christmas at sea.'

'Very. Sometimes I wonder whose side God's on.'

'You're not alone there, nurse.' The distress in her tone made him sound terse. 'About this piano. I know one we can have. I'll have a word about it with Sister in the morning. Thanks for the tip. Anything else you want me for?'

Rose looked down her nose and said primly, 'No, thank you, Mr Arden.'

'Good.' He rose quickly. 'Don't shift. 'Night, nurse.'

'Goodnight, Mr Arden,' she said to his back and when the hall curtains closed behind him, she shook her head at her thoughts, then reached for her torch and stood up to do another round of her sleeping patients.

Johnny wasn't sleeping and turned his head as she slowly approached his bed, holding her skirts to her sides to prevent the starch rustling and as she moved from bed to bed directing her torch beam from the shoulders to the feet of the sleepers. The reflected glow allowed her to see their face without waking them. A torchbeam in the face woke most patients of either sex and, unless in coma, all that had been fighting men.

'Awake long?' She switched off the torch and put it on his locker to shake up his pillows.

146

'Few minutes,' he lied, then gave it away. 'Why the long heart-to-heart with J.J.?'

She could see well enough in the darkness to see his shaving mirror. She glanced at it covertly and gave him some of the truth. 'In case he can't scrounge the one he's got in mind, keep this dark.'

'You have to ask me to keep my big mouth shut?' He looked up at her and as it was too dark even for her to see his expression, all the truth was in his eyes. 'Am I a heel, period. Christ knows you rate the seventy-six, and I'm wishing to hell Night Sister or someone'll scrap it for you.'

She was intentionally light. 'Be one hell of a family row if I can't make town tomorrow. My mother-in-law's down till Christmas Eve. It's over a year since our last meeting and oh, the planning that's gone into this one.'

'Guess so.' He tried to keep it light. 'What's she like?'

'Sweet, in small doses. She was a very pretty sub-blonde – still is very pretty. Kirby-type, but only physically. Michael Kirby's ops and MO 1 started Kirby growing up fast. My mother-in-law never has and that was quite a break for her when Stephen was killed as she never really let herself take it in. She doesn't like discussing or facing what she calls "sad things" "Let's talk of happy things, dear." ' She smiled wryly. 'Not her fault. Her husband and three sons – Stephen too – have always loved treating her as if she's made of glass and ten years old. She's a good wife and mother and she's always been sweet to me.'

'I'll bet!' he muttered grimly.

She ignored that. 'When we meet tomorrow, she'll say as she's said or written every time I've gone on nights, "I'm so glad you're on night duty, dear. You need a little rest and, of course, everyone sleeps at night, don't they?" '

He slapped a hand over his mouth to stifle his involuntary laugh. 'Tried suggesting she tells that one to the Marines?'

'If I did she'd go out and look for a Marine. Hush. Like a drink?'

'No, thanks. Not thirsty. What I'd like –' he reached for

her left hand and his grip made her wedding ring hurt her finger. 'Christ,' he breathed 'do I envy that poor dead sod.'

'Don't kid yourself, Johnny.' She spoke under her breath and very firmly. 'For all its hell, you enjoy life too much really to wish you'd been dead three-and-half years. You enjoy life because you've got stupendous guts. You know it. I know it. Everyone that knows you, knows it. Your-type guts don't just help you, helps us all, so do me a favour. If we get a piano –' she jerked her head at Sam Eccles's bed 'go into action on him. Deal?'

He released her hand and for a few moments looked up at her in silence. 'We heroic types, nursie, need strong char from those attempting to twist our arms. Slip me a cocoa or a hot milk or the deal's off.'

'I'm about to brew-up on the double.'

'Make it a dead run. Just discovered I am thirsty.'

She waved in answer, switched on her torch and he watched the pool of light moving over the floor, her slight, narrow-waisted back, and the white wings of the bow above her black bun. No new discovery, he thought wearily, and by Christ, am I bloody thirsty.

Sister MO 1 fractionally readjusted the lace bow under her chin. 'The carol-singing was remarkably good tonight. Some of those probationers had really good voices. They reached us at twenty-past eight. A little early, perhaps, but as they have to be all round the hospital by 10.30 and geographical convenience places us third call, the timing was unavoidable. As usual, we turned off the main lights for their visit and with their cloaks reversed and torches and cycle lamps illuminating the scarlet linings, when the fifty-odd pairs filed in singing, the effect was not unimpressive.'

Curiouser and curiouser, thought Rose, She's not chatting for nothing. Something's coming. 'What carols did our patients choose, Sister?' she asked, guessing the answer.

'Hark The Herald,' 'God Rest Ye Merry,' and 'Oh Come All Ye Faithful.'

On target, thought Rose, and no prizes, seeing this is my fourth in hospital. And that last was a dead cert. Every Christmas, every male ward wanted 'Oh Come All Ye Faithful' and every female ward, 'Away In A Manger,' just as, for the weekly ward services the men demanded and bellowed out 'Onward Christian Soldiers' and the women, 'Abide With Me,' that invariably had the whole ward in tears before it ended. But those tears were very different to the unshed tears in the eyes of men and women patients when the voices of the filing-out, carol-singing pros faded from the darkened wards and left in their wake a short silence that had always seemed to Rose the saddest of the whole hospital year. Was that because of the war? Not having nursed in peacetime, she couldn't be sure, but thought it very likely the war. Carols, Christmas, home and peace were so deeply associated and entrenched in the British psychology that even the atheists and the agnostics had difficulty in ignoring inherited traditions when lying in hospital beds listening to carols on Christmas Eve. Five, she thought, remembering Joe's words, five. How many more? We've all long stopped asking that one. One year the war'll be over. One year the Second Front'll start. Not this year now. Next year – sometime – never – no, not 'never' now the Yanks are over here and thank God that they are and for their industrial wealth and millions of men that unlike ours, haven't been fighting for four years.

She said, 'I'm sure the patients appreciated the carols, Sister, but it is rather a pity we were an early call. It's so much easier for the patients if, a few minutes after the singers leave, they can be settled for the night. Were they – er – very glum, afterwards?'

'Glum, Nurse Weston, is an unprofessional word. In low spirits, would have been more suitable. I do not approve of the use of slang to which your generation is lamentably prone.' The stern retort was mitigated by the ghost of a smile in the lined, dramatically dark eyes. 'Nevertheless, a nurse's ability to speak the same language as her patients is often of great mutual benefit and you and Nurse Ashley-Ellis share the generation of most of our

149

patients tonight. Just close that door properly for a few moments, please, nurse.'

My God, what've I done? Johnny? Flashed through Rose's mind as she leapt to the door. When she turned Sister had risen and was unlocking her private stores cupboard.

The small dutyroom was crammed with large deal cupboards containing medicines, lotions, plaster bandages, stock, (clean but unsterile dressings, that, as always, were made in the ward by the day nurses), and slightly smaller, invariably locked, Schedule A and Dangerous Drug, and Sister's private, cupboards. Between the cupboards were wall shelves stacked with the patients' old notes and X-rays, spare temperature charts, case history sheets, pathological and other request forms, orthopaedic and medical textbooks, and on the top shelves were the ward's one X-ray screen, blood-pressure machine, stethoscope, patella hammer and, stacked high on their own portion, today's emptied dressing-drums that Nurse Ashley-Ellis would refill from the stock cupboard during tonight and early tomorrow, as on every morning in the year, would be collected by a day porter from the Surgical Stores that housed the hospital's autoclave.

Rose's wide eyes opened wide.

Sister placed methodically on the table a bottle of whisky, one of gin, and a smaller bottle of 'maternity' concentrated orange juice, then relocked her cupboard. 'The whisky is a present to the ward from Mr Arden; the gin, from Mr Hodges. The orange juice,' she went on without a flicker of emotion, 'I obtained from other sources. I had intended saving these for tomorrow, but early this afternoon the Americans' Commanding Officer most kindly presented me with a bottle of Bourbon for my patients, and then Mrs Stamford called with one of the bottles of her elderflower wine that she generously gives us every year. Between ourselves, nurse, that wine has the kick of raw cider. A little goes a very long way. So I think we can spare these for nightcaps tonight.'

Rose's eyes were alight with laughter but she kept her

tone suitably grave, 'I'm sure you're right, Sister.'

'So Messrs Hodges and Arden agreed earlier. They came in together just after Mrs Stamford left. Naturally, both surgeons are resident in the hospital tonight.' She paused a moment. 'I had a very pleasant chat with Mrs Stamford. She mentioned your late grandfather. I wasn't until then aware you were Sir Henry's granddaughter. I was only slightly acquainted with him during his long tenure as one of our Governors, but I found him most pleasant and he was a most valuable friend of St Martha's.'

Rose had stiffened. How the hell did Mrs Stamford – be your age, Rosie, she reminded herself furiously, too easy if she read pre-war gossip columns and had a weakness for glossy society magazines and a good memory for faces and names. She was always pottering in and out of the hut wards writing letters for the men, or talking to them. She was a friendly, chatty old soul – and as she'd have called all round the hospital today – hell, hell, hell! Joe was bound to – hold it – had he already? That night Bevis died – the night before Kirby left – tea – in here – was that why? – lay off, Rosie! Not now! She said politely, 'I'm glad, Sister. Nightcaps all round?'

Sister was amused. 'You are indeed Sir Henry's grand-daughter, nurse. He had the reputation of unfailingly keeping to the matter in hand. Yes. It's Christmas Eve and time for a little cheerfulness to break in. The senior surgeons have told me there will be no night rounds here before eleven. When I leave here, I shall go straight to the Office to inform Night Sister that I have given you one hour's extension of lights off – yes, you may keep them on until eleven – and request that she delays her first round until after that hour. Get them settled for the night by then. Until then, cheer them up, and if you see fit, try the piano for us. Captain Eccles has been back in bed since his evening wash, but another half-hour or so in a chair could benefit him and his fellows. They're all very concerned about that young man and they have enough concerns of their own to bear. Do what you can for them, nurse.'

Training, old habit and the prospect of MO 1's reaction

when she pushed in the medicine trolley in a few minutes time, thrust all else to the back of Rose's mind. 'I will, Sister, or rather, we will.'

'Yes. Nurse Ashley-Ellis is a sensible gel. You may open that door now, please, Nurse Weston.'

Once she had seen Sister out, Rose raced to the kitchen. First drinks had gone round and Midget at the stove was stirring the cocoa for second cups as he hung over one armpit crutch and listened with a painfully polite expression to a story Jill Ashley-Ellis said would have him in positive stitches if only she was better at telling funny stories. '. . . so this chap got to Heaven and St Peter said to him – no, he said to St Peter, "I've got me best whites and me best halo but I've not got no best wings seeing as the bloke with the halo down the Quartermaster's Stores says" – no, it wasn't to St Peter it was to –' she broke off. 'Wanting a hand, nurse?'

'Please, Corp.' Rose glanced at Midget. Looks just like a schoolboy forced to stay on at school for the holidays whilst all the rest've gone home, she noted and mentally hugged Sister. 'Turn off that cocoa, Mr Duncan.'

'Not boiling yet –'

'Not to worry. Not needed.' She smiled up at him. 'Do me a favour. Go back into the ward, spring some excuse for seconds being late and on the quiet tip off Mr Player that sharpish I want him and you to go into action. The medicine trolley's the signal. He'll catch on.'

'But – Sister's done evening medicines, nurse –'

'Yes, Mr Duncan.' She flapped her eyelashes at him. 'I know she has. But I've got some more medicine for MO 1 and as you'll know, being a Scot, some medicines are nicer than others.' She laughed at the dawning understanding in his smooth, fair, boyish face. 'If you breathe one word about this bit before we're ready, I'll bust that good leg with my two hands.'

He flushed with excitement. 'Party on?'

'And how! Get going – hey, watch that leg, man! Gently does it!'

Jill spluttered, 'Nurse, I'm positively agog! What gives?'

152

'Bring every glass you can find in here and a large jug of drinking water into the dutyroom and you'll see.' Rose shot on for the glass-shelved medicine trolley and two red-and-white check table cloths. She had draped them over the glass when Jill came in and nearly dropped her laden tray.

'Zowie, nurse! Who coughed 'em up?'

'Our pundits and Lease-Lend.' Rose brandished the orange juice. 'Sister, as usual, is upholding Martha's traditions in the wilderness. Since the Yanks started sending this stuff over, it-and-gin have been the traditional tipple at all Martha's parties. Let's have those glasses – oh! You do realise you and I are on the wagon, period?'

'Golly, yes! Jolly G thing, actually. One sniff of a barmaid's apron and I'm stinkeroo. I say, how about a spot of holly on the trolley?'

'Bright wheeze. Can you grab some without their noticing?'

'Cloak-and-dagger, can do.' Jill strode for the hall, muttering, 'Where did I drop my scissors? Coming in, perchance –?' she dived through the hall curtains, dislodging a bunch of holly and thrusting it in her dress skirt pocket.

Midget, sitting on the end of the empty 21, exchanged deadpan glances with Johnny and both avoided looking at her. The others did so briefly and incuriously.

MO 1 was growing fond of the Corp and thought her a damned nice type, but just looking at her didn't automatically make the world seem less intolerable. Intolerable as hell tonight, decided MO 1, in gloomy self-disgust over feeling so bloodyminded after all the sweat Sister and the day nurses had put into making the damned paperchains out of crepe paper and flour-and-water paste, and dolling up the damned tree with cotton-wool snow-balls, handmade, hand-painted cardboard stars and re-dressing with surgical gauze touched up with silver paint Sister had scrounged from somewhere, the damned fairy on the top. At least the tree had provided today's one good belly laugh when Sister had powdered it with Epsom's Salts in lieu of artificial frost. That aside, the sooner today was over the better, as even although bloody grateful, MO 1 was so browned off with life in general and this farce in particular, that it was fried to a bloody crisp. Tomorrow was going to be even more hideous what with the pundits horsing round carving the turkey, afternoon visitors for those sods lucky enough to have folks living near enough to come in, which was bloody few, and not even the hope of a hangover to make it bearable. 'You'll all have a little something before luncheon tomorrow, gentlemen,' said Sister serving lunches today. God give a chap strength! He bloody needed it to survive Christmas in hospital. Remember last year's – oh, bloody skip it and have another fag . . .

'Corp, you're a genius. How's that?'

'Positively jolly. I say – having another brainwave – could we pin sprigs to our caps? Or that only allowed on Christmas Day?'

'Officially. So what? Sister wants a little cheerfulness to break in. Right. Get fell in for cheerfulness, Corp.' They broke off and pinned small sprigs to their respective caps. 'If Night Sister does show up for an early round, stand by with the oxygen as she'll undoubtedly have a coronary, but she'll probably be late as Sister MO 1 scares the living daylights out of her and every other Sister in this hospital. Talking of oxygen, remind me later that I've just thought how we can turn some of the cylinders into a platoon of Father Christmases with red blankets, cotton wool and bolster cases stuffed with anything we can lay hands on.'

'Roger, nurse!' Jill surveyed the decorated trolley. 'Just wish we'd some ice for the chaps.'

Momentarily, Rose looked at the floor. Lay off it, she insisted to herself. Lay off it, *stat*. Looking back anywhere is always a mistake. Looking back in a ward or in a war on this night – worse than a mistake. She looked up and smiled. 'Not to worry, Corp.' She jerked a thumb. 'British troops in there, not Yanks. Let's go.'

Three seconds later Midget, Johnny, and George Hall – now in the secret – let out in unison the British equivalent of the American Confederate Army's Rebel Yell that in less than a second was backed by Major Chalmers sounding 'Gone awaay' on his hunting horn. MO 1 slapped down reading materials and exploded into party mood before the glasses were in the outstretched hands. Well within the next thirty minutes the nurses had lifted Sam Eccles into a wheelchair held steady by Midget, the chair was at the piano, and whilst almost unnoticed the nurses rubbed backs, elbows, ankles and heels and pulled through draw-sheets and turned pillows, the brick walls of the villa vibrated with the singing and clapping of 'Deep In The Heart Of Texas', 'Pistol Packin' Momma', 'The Darktown Strutters Ball' and similar numbers from Sam's apparently limitless, near-professional repertoire.

The whole ward was asleep and Mr Hodges and Night Sister had come and gone, when, between 1.0 and 2.0, the nurses silently moved the tree that was potted in a fire bucket, into the middle of the hall and converted one line of spare cylinders into small, guardsmen-straight, Father Christmases. And then, taking opposite sides of the long ward, they went soundlessly from bed to bed, and hung the filled operation stockings to the top footrails. In the stockings were cigarettes and soap from the Ward Fund, apples from Mr Brunton to replace the wartime non-existent oranges in the toes, and any presents from their relatives that could be fitted in. The larger parcels went on the locker tops, but owing to rationing and shortages, these were few; no man had more than one and several of the single men, had none.

Night Sister was early for her second round. 'Is my report ready, nurse? Oh. Thank you. They all seem to be sleeping quite nicely.'

'Yes, Sister.'

'The whole hospital is fairly quiet tonight. All the men have now gone to bed. Even the physicians. I'm glad. Tomorrow is a heavy day for the men and as the weather at sea appears to be improving from Matron's report tonight, we may well have our next convoy in before your set leaves us on the 29th. But I mustn't dawdle. The rain has stopped and the moon is trying to break through, but the clouds are still low and heavy.'

And it's being so cheerful that keeps you going, thought Rose. She said smiling, 'Thank you, Sister, and a Happy Christmas.'

Night Sister smiled perfunctorily. Her gastric ulcer was nagging. 'Thank you, nurse. And to you.' She hooked her cloak collar and bustled out into the cold, damp, black silence of the country night.

Rose returned to her chair at the desk and unconsciously stifled a yawn. This afternoon she had got back to the Night Home in time to be in bed by 3.0, that was the bedtime deadline for nurses returning from nights off that was rigorously enforced by the Night Home Sister. Rose had only slept for about an hour and spent the remaining time facing reality and what seemed insoluble problems. I don't just go for Joe Arden, she'd thought, and I haven't just fallen for him. I love him and I want to spend the rest of my life with him as I know the more I see of him, the more I'll love him. In some ways, and certainly physically, he's very like Stephen – or rather, he's very like my darling Stephen could've been if he'd had time to reach Joe's age and learnt how to control his curly hair, long legs and hands and feet. He was as gangling as Midget and didn't look much older, but inside he was as solid as Joe and if his father hadn't been at school with mine and grandfather hadn't been all for it and tactful as hell about my marriage settlement, Stephen wouldn't have married me. He wouldn't touch my allowance and I had to be tactful as hell about using it, but as he was so much younger than Joe I was able to handle things. Joe I wouldn't attempt to handle even if I could, which I can't. I still don't even know where he hails from, but it ought to be Sussex as he can't be drove. And I love him for it even though he now seems to have lost all interest in me and when I come off nights and get shifted back to London, that will be that, period. How can it be anything else? What can I do? I must do something – I can't – but I must – only how can I? and – what?

Sitting at the desk she no longer felt tired. She had moved into that curious limbo that lies beyond fatigue and in which the overactive brain sees into problems with a crystal clarity. What I must do about Joe and my life, she thought, is what all of us will have to do until this damned war ends and that's sweat out whatever the book turns up. I can't bear the thought of leaving him, or MO 1, but I'll have to leave both before this year ends, just as, soon as we're over Hospital Finals, our set'll have to leave Martha's before our fourth year ends. The Forces are so hungry for newly trained nurses that once all the exams are over, we'll all get sucked in. By this time next year, most of us'll be wearing Army sisters' caps and nursing the men overseas. And Joe – will still be here. And some of the men we'll send home, will come here and some of those will have their first, and quite possibly their second Christmas here, even if we keep up this new order of winning our battles. Jolly good show, chaps and don't – don't – she thought passionately, look at what's left on the battlefield. Any battlefield.

But things like that, you know, must be,
After a famous victory.

Oh no, chaps, she thought, oh no, don't look round the battlefield. Just take a good look round MO 1 in the small hours of Christmas '43 –

A sound interrupted her thoughts and she listened to it absently from force of new habit. And then, from an old and almost forgotten habit, she listened more intently. It was the sound of a solitary aircraft and still too distant to disturb even the lightest sleeper, and what disturbed her about it was more than the faintly troubled note of its engine.

It can't be, she thought rapidly, it can't be! Not down here. He's never come anywhere near here. But already her reflexes had jerked her to her feet. Like hell it can't be! It is! It's one of his!

9

'Jerry?' echoed Jill, outraged. One was more than happy to do one's bit for the chaps and take the rough with the smooth but Jerry upstairs in the early hours of Christmas morning was positively the giddy limit! And, let's face it, jolly unlikely. 'Sorry and all that, nurse, but couldn't he be one of ours stooging round for the FTS? Or a Flying Fort. that's turned sharp left instead of sharp right?'

'Yanks don't do night raids and I'll lay my last bob he's not ours. Got the Jerry-throb.' Rose, in the kitchen doorway, stared up at the cracked, steamy ceiling, her ears straining and mind racing.

Why hadn't he come closer or disappeared? On reconnaissance? Off-course? Instruments or R/T and W/T gone U/S (unserviceable) or couldn't be used over enemy territory without giving away his position? Kirby said there were times when ours couldn't use theirs – and what was that bit she'd said about Jerry having a beam? Had he lost his beam? Jerry? Who, everyone said made superb machines – not superb enough to beat our Spits. in '40 or stop his cities from being blitzed all this year – but one thing they all say is that he's a fighting man. He now fighting back over here? Lost his way home after a raid on some port or London tonight that we wouldn't know about yet? He sounds a long-range bomber – I know that throb – and if he's still got his bombs he'll want to drop them before he beats it for the French coast – and have to drop them before he lands. And I think he wants to land. From the sound, he's circling. He's coming and going and each come is about the same distance as the last. And if he's having to rely on sight he's looking for a break in the clouds to drop his load on something worth hitting rather than risk wasting them on open country as that's what any fighting man would do though he must know that every minute he's up there he's risking the lives of his crew, himself and his aircraft. If the clouds do break, or he gets down under them and sees our Nissen and wooden huts he could mistake us for a camp – he wouldn't know we're a hospital – and if he did, why should he give a damn? Seeing how many hospitals he's already totally or half-flattened in London alone?

Jill, continuing cutting the breakfast bread, eyed her speculatively. Not like Rosie W. to go off at half-cock but she had been on nights over three months. Tactful reminder might do the job. 'The alert hasn't gone, nurse.'

Rose looked at her. 'Okay. If I'm flapping, I'm flapping. We're not waiting. We'll get Williams off his blocks, all the men against the outside wall into the middle, and shove spare pillows onto their bedcradles. We'll use the pillows on the empties. They've all enough pillows already to cover their faces and heads and as going flat on their faces is agony for all but Sam, we'll just do him. Anyway, tractions and spinals we can't turn. We'll leave Midget but if the alert goes, he must get under his bed, you stick with Williams and I'll stick with Sam. He's our most helpless tonight – oh yes, and I'll cope with the ether bottles.' She spoke quietly and very quickly. 'We'll try not to wake 'em. On the double, Corp.' She vanished.

Jill stuck the breadknife into the loaf and charged in pursuit. Hers not to reason why, hers but to – I say, steady on, upstairs! Much nearer and you'll wake the chaps! That's the form. Making tracks again – or, was he?

They worked swiftly in a slightly breathless silence whilst around them MO 1 slept on, snoring, grunting, sighing, breathing deeply and rhythmically and far above them the fading and returning growling grew gently louder. All the eight bedpatients backed against the outside wall were in mid-ward and Williams's bed was off its foot-blocks, when the piercing, single-noted wail of the hospital's siren sounding 'air-raid alert' woke every man.

The circling aircraft was still high above the low cloud base and for the last several minutes the telephones had been ringing in the nearest military camps, the RAF FTS and the local ARP posts. Two Lancaster bombers returning from tonight's raids on Germany badly shot-up had been seen limping over the Channel, but had not yet returned to base or made further contact and their whereabouts were unknown. 'Till those clouds shift enough to tell if he's ours or a Jerry,' the Avonly ARP warden on night-duty told his telephone operator-cum-fellow fire-watcher, 'no saying and no shooting, seems. As well, if you asks me, seeing what goes up must come down. If the ack-ack starts taking pot-shots or gets jackpot, no three guesses where the lot'll fall. Give Everly Place the word, Ted.'

'Nice little Christmas present for the hospital,' observed Ted, jiggling the metal holder of his trumpet-shaped receiver to attract the attention of the night operator at the local telephone exchange. 'Not right.'

'War's not, mate, as I should know seeing I gone for a soldier in the last do. A right mucky do, that was. This lot don't know their luck.'

Keep going, you bastard, keep going, thought Rose furiously, racing from burying the ether bottles lined on a shelf outside the sterilising room, in the sand-filled fire buckets in the West End passage. On her return to the ward, she grabbed pillows from the empty beds and had to raise her voice, 'Sorry you've been woken, gentlemen. Get your heads flat down, pillows over your faces and hang on to at least the bottom pillow. Extra pillows coming.' She deposited pillow after pillow on the Brigadier and in the West End then ran on to join Jill doing the same in the East. 'Catch, Mr Player!'

He caught the pillow, nimbly. 'And a very happy Christmas to you too, nursie!'

'And to you and all of you – get your head down under, man! Ready, Corp?' They were either side of Sam Eccles. 'Over you go, captain. That's it.' They heaped pillows over the back of his head and neck. 'Hang on to the corners of the bottom – good –' Rose dived for Midget. 'Wakey, wakey, up and under your bed. I'll take your bad leg – that's it.' The siren had stopped and the growling was much louder. She didn't have to tell him to lie on his face and as she hauled off his blankets and pillows and thrust them over him she was thankful that he, at least, had the added protection of the bedsprings, fracture boards and mattress above him. 'Williams, Corp!' She leapt across the ward to check the spinals as Jill vanished. 'Got enough air to breathe, you two?'

George Hall's muffled voice sounded as if he was smiling. 'Snug but lonely, nursie. Couldn't you cuddle up a little closer, nursie?'

'Some other time, captain.' She leapt back to Sam Eccles.

'Lecherous sod, that's what you are, George,' announced Johnny, remembering his shaving mirror and reaching blindly for it with his left hand to lower it to safety under his bed. 'But after that damned good party, I forgive you.' He suddenly realised his locker was well behind him, and using both hands on his headrails to haul himself closer to them and extend his reach, he sang out, 'Oh, tidings of comfort and joy – comfort and joy – oh, oh, tidings of com –' his voice was suddenly drowned by the roar of the aircraft diving under the clouds. And then they all heard a thin, shrill, whistle.

Only Jill failed to recognise that whistle. Every man shouted 'Down, nurses!' and Rose, 'Down, Corp!' Rose had positioned herself between Sam and Midget to face her whole ward and as she shouted she flung her body from the waist face down over Sam's buried head and shoulders and instinctively grabbed with her left hand the lowest rung of his headrail and with her right his farside bedrail to steady herself against what must come.

Jill was standing on Williams's right to face the ward and her momentary hesitation was overcome by his swinging arm that knocked her off her feet and half under his bed. She hit the floor as the first bomb exploded.

It fell on the cement road between MO 1 and Main Block; the second exploded on the ambulances' yard that had once been a spacious lawn; the third, just beyond the hardboard partitioned Nissen hut that housed the resident and temporary resident medical staff, that stood roughly fifty yards to the right of and a little higher than Main Block and backed into the wood above. In around and perhaps under four seconds from that first whistle, the German long-range bomber crashed into the hilltop and exploded into flames.

The repeated onslaughts of noise and blast literally shook the villa to its brick foundations and so stunned minds, senses and reflexes that the pain it caused in unhealed bones and tissues and in ears, teeth and heads, went as unnoticed as the splintering of glass, the crashing down of blackout screens, the clatter of rocking lockers emptying their contents onto the ward floor and of enamel urinals, bedpans, washing basins, shaving bowls, mouthwash mugs falling from their racks and shelves in the East End sluice and the tiles shooting off the roof like machine-gunfire.

Being the closer to the bombs' points of impact, and especially the first two, the East End took the greater onslaught of the blast, but, as so often, this was erratic. It blew in the small, high windows and blackout screens in the empty SWs 3 and 4 and ripped the red-padding from their window walls; it stripped the filled operation stockings from the East End's inside, but not middle beds and left untouched all in the West End; it removed all the tree's decorations, but left the tree upright in its sand-filled fire bucket; it flung down the screen covering the hall passage and the two half-open at the entrance to the West End, but not the pair at the East End's entrance; it flung the card-table desk down on one side, and emptied the red and black inkwells onto the floor without cracking their glass. It brought down every West End blackout screen, but only shattered the window behind and to the right of Major Chalmers and embedded with glass splinters the area of floor covered by the top half of his high bed when in its rightful place. It only half-dislodged one blackout screen in the main body of the East End when it tore a jagged hole through glass and antiblast paper strips in the window between 18 and 19 and strewed with glass splinters both empty beds that were still against the outer wall.

It had been the second bomb that had put out every mains electricity light in the hospital, but when finally the noise subsided, no one in MO 1 knew just when the red-shaded hall light and its passage lights had gone out. It took a few seconds before the stunned senses dared trust the new silence enough to blink open eyes and accept the blackness in the ward for what it was and not blindness.

Rose pushed herself upright with shaking hands and, staggering a little on her feet, was immediately aware of a face-level current of cold air smelling of explosives, burning, smoke, cement dust and fresh-flung up earth and reaching into the East End like an evil, dead, arm. She fumbled for the torch in her dress pocket and called clearly, but in the voice of an old woman, 'Anyone hurt? East? West? Brigadier? Corp?'

The answers came in deep-throated, deeply gasping, mutters, 'Fine, thanks. You all right, nurse? Corp?'

'I'm fine, thanks. You're all sure?' Rose insisted sounding more middle-aged than old. 'How about you, Corp?'

'One piece.' Jill rose unsteadily from the floor guided by Major Williams's outstretched hand. 'Bit winded.' Her voice quavered with shock. 'Dropped my torch but I think our blackouts up here've all gone for a Burton.' She found her torch. 'Still okay. Jolly G.'

'Good.' Rose had flicked on her torch and the light was on Sam Eccles. He had pushed away the shielding pillows and lay flat, with his white face towards the West End, panting like a helpless, stranded fish. He lifted his left hand weakly to show he was all right. Rose caught his hand and it was so cold that she held it whilst shining her light under Midget's bed. Midget waved and began edging out on his elbows.

'Stay put till the all-clear, Mr Duncan as –'

'Sorry, nursie. Forgot.' He edged back.

Jill was swinging the beam of her torch round the West End. 'All well up here but blackouts down.'

'Get 'em back up if you can and if you can't shove up open brown screens and watch that light, Corp. Can't hear more but he could've had a chum upstairs – no!' Rose's voice sounded her own in her relief at the undulating wail of the all-clear. Thank God he didn't get MO 1 and don't think – *don't think* – what may've happened to Main Block, anywhere else, or – him. MO 1 needs me so much right now, she thought in fast-motion, but no more than I need them, right now. She went on calmly, 'Jerry obviously got our mains, but our emergency generators'll have the lights back soon. Tea all round then. We'll get you all settled more comfortably whilst we're waiting.' Whilst speaking and still holding Sam's hand, she swung her torchlight from bedhead to bedhead up the inner side then down the five beds in the middle. In bed after bed, the white, drawn, shocked faces of the wounded men, blinked painfully in the beam that in that darkness seemed strong as a searchlight, then smiled painfully and closed their eyes and lay flat on their backs too exhausted to push under their heads even one of their thrust aside mounds of pillows. Only when the beam reached the final pulled-out bed was there no blinking and no twisting of bloodless lips into a forced smile. Johnny's white lips were fixed in a faint smile; all his pillows were on the floor and his unblinking eyes were staring at the ceiling.

The torchbeam wavered, and then became a streak of light over the floor between Sam and Johnny's bedheads. Then, with her back blocking Johnny's face from George Hall, she illuminated Johnny for a second or two that seemed to her endless, then switched out the light. In the blackness she laid one hand on the already cold forehead, held the other flattened just over the lifeless lips, then slid her hand inside the pyjama jacket and against the cold stilled chest above the silenced heart. She had known this must be from her first agonised glimpse from Sam's bedside. She had seen death too often not to recognise

164

immediately the unmistakable look of the newly dead and looked upon that look more often than she could bear, or dared to recall. But standing by Johnny's body in that shrouding darkness with the evil-smelling icy current hitting her agonised face, for the only time in her nursing career she very nearly fainted on duty.

The combination of her training and a violent upsurge of her adrenalin saved her from fainting. She was suddenly consumed with an anger she had never before suspected she was capable of harbouring and that was of the calibre that had inspired some men to win the Victoria Cross. The entire crew of the German bomber had been killed outright when their plane had hit the hill, but if it had been possible in that moment for one of them to have come into MO 1, she would have tried to kill him and not improbably succeeded by using as a dagger either her scissors, or one of the longish jagged slivers of glass lying on the clean white quilts of 18 and 19.

No glass had fallen on Johnny's bed, but he had gripped the headrails for the single second too long that had been all the blast needed to remove his pillows and his life. A flying sliver of glass roughly four inches long and half-an-inch wide had pierced him between the eyes so deeply that less than one-tenth of an inch remained visible and killed him so swiftly that only a few drops of blood had coalesced into a small clot over the kink in his nose that had been made by a cricket ball a few weeks after he left school when he wore his first County Cap in the summer of 1938.

Rose hitched out her watch and held its face in her hand-guarded torchlight. 2.20. Night Sister had left between 2.05 and 2.10. Impossible! Oh no. Oh no. Not in war.

Again she switched off the light and, in the darkness that seemed to have penetrated every cell in her brain and body, she gently closed Johnny's eyes and straightened to his sides the limp arms lying with the palms of the hands uppermost, between the headrails. Then she covered his face with the turn-down of his top sheet and in a voice as detached and cold as her own hands felt to her, she said clearly, 'I must get that blackout up over the broken window this end.'

Again her torchbeam made a streaking light on the floor but this time followed by Sam Eccles's eyes. His face was set and rigid as he took the new blow with his customary quietude. He had sensed the truth when she had suddenly gripped tightly then dropped his hand and twisted his head over his shoulder in time to glimpse Johnny's face before she turned off the torch. She had seen sudden death too often, but not as often as he had at Salerno, in Sicily, in North Africa, in France.

She had reached the broken window and held the lighted torch with her teeth whilst she reclipped in place the dislodged but otherwise undamanged screen. Then the torch was back in her hand and she quickly opened, illuminated the interiors, then closed the doors of both small wards. Sam guessed she had hoped to move Johnny's bed into one until his body was ready to leave the ward, and why this was impossible, and what might have happened had those small wards been occupied tonight. He wasted no time on that last speculation. What-might-have-been had become a forbidden expression to his mental vocabulary.

She had moved on to the stacked old brown screens temporarily removed from the hall. She thrust her lighted torch inside her apron bib to lift two screens together and the torch blurred with light the front of her body and made it appear headless and legless. When she opened the first screen between George Hall and Johnny's beds, Sam heard George's urgent, 'What the hell – ?' and Midget's gasped 'Johnny – ?' in the same second that the hall curtains were thrust aside, a powerful beam split the darkness and J.J.'s voice called, 'All right in MO 1? Anyone hurt?'

Before Rose could answer or properly believe it was Joe's voice, Sam called back in a stronger and more authoritative voice than anyone present had heard him use before, 'All well but Johnny, sir. He's bought it. Nurse Weston's by his bed.'

Rose had emerged from the screens and as the powerful

torchlight caught her face, she paused and instinctively closed her eyes. And to the tight-lipped, tight-faced men in their beds on either side and to Midget, sitting on the side of his stripped bed with no trace of boyishness in his young face, Rose's white-faced white figure, with her blast-flattened cap lying like a wilted lily on the crown of her black head, had the ethereal quality of a frail, exhausted, ghost. But to Joe Arden's smoke-reddened eyes still glazed by his fear of finding her dead, her slight figure seemed to have shrunk and her face to have aged years, and she had about her a heartbreaking aura of her awareness of the waste of so much courage, of the uselessness of so much suffering, and of the helplessness of humans when humanity itself goes mad.

He lowered the light and she moved quickly to him. 'Main Block? The rest of the hospital?'

'All other wards intact, aside from the lights. They're getting going on our emergency generators now. Lights'll be on, shortly.' He spoke for all to hear and had consciously to control his tone, his breathing, his wonder that she was alive, and the pain of his despair for Johnny. He had just run from Main Block the fastest sprint of his adult life and until he had cleared the first bomb's crater, dust and smoke, he had thought MO 1 had had a direct hit. 'Your phone's down, nurse.' He dropped his voice to a murmur. 'Just Johnny?'

'Yes.'

'One moment.' He ducked back through the undamaged battened entrance doors, shouted MO 1's general situation to the senior night porter, who was the nearest member of the hastily formed rescue squad, then ducked back into the hall. 'Repairs and Works'll have an emergency phone set and cable to you soon. All the hut lines are functioning. Thomas and Lomax have gone straight to the huts, Hodges has gone to FO 1.' Again, he dropped his voice. 'How?'

She told him quietly and kept her voice steady. She didn't know how she managed that. She added, 'I hadn't had time to tell them. Sam must'ved seen –' she broke off, then forced herself to go on. 'I've not yet got in there.' She swung her torch beam over the West End. Six hands were raised to her and Major Chalmers called tonelessly, 'The Brigadier's fine, nurse. Eh, sir?'

'Yes, thanks, Charlie – nurse!' responded the Brigadier briskly and in the privacy of his dark small ward he sighed silently and sadly.

'Good,' said Joe as if on a normal ward round. He wore his old duffle coat open over sweater and trousers pulled on over pyjamas, and his bare feet were in wellingtons, the quickest footwear to put on and best civilian foot protection against the broken glass that inevitably strewed floors, pavements and roads after air attacks. It was too dark for Rose to see the dust and grime on his coat, shock-haggard face and untidy hair, but in the numbness that had now swamped all her emotions, she noticed the corner of his pyjama collar sticking up from the neck of his sweater and thought, as I can't believe any of this yet I can't yet believe that he's alive.

He said very gently, 'Nurse, I must see Johnny then get on to the huts. I'll be back, later.'

'Yes, Mr Arden.' He had to see Johnny to confirm his death and come back later to sign the death certificate. The second could wait, not the first as it had been a sudden unexpected death. It was a hospital rule and the law that when this occurred a doctor must give the final, official confirmation as soon as possible and both rules were as unbreakable as the one that ordained that the night senior performed the Last Offices when a patient in her charge died at night. A patient, or patients. One night earlier this year when she had been in charge of a Martha's Hut male ward as a third-year relief senior, three patients had died. She had never forgotten that terrible night. She would never forget this one. Or, Johnny. Never.

They were by his screened bed when the hall and passage lights flickered then came on steadily. Beyond the open brown screens in comparison with the previous blackness the reddish darkness was akin to the first belated light of the mid-winter dawn sky. But in the shadows of the screens they needed their torchlights and Rose's was growing pale from over-use. Neither spoke, and when Joe pulled off the stethoscope that only the law demanded he use, they recovered together the thin, faintly smiling, closed-eyed face that death had already youthened to that of a boy. And then for about a minute they stood on either side of the bed with their heads lowered and in the silence that enveloped the whole East End.

Joe moved to the foot of the bed and waited. She joined him slowly without looking up. 'He knew nothing, nurse.'

She nodded, too sad for speech or tears.

He hesitated, then rested one hand lightly on her shoulder. 'SW3?'

She had to answer. 'I'd thought of that. Help the others. Can't. Both SWs've had it. He must stay here, till –'

'Yes.' His hand on her shoulder tightened, then fell to his side. 'I must get on to the huts. I'll be back soon as I can make it.'

She looked up then and in the reflected light from his downward directed torch he saw the distress, the desperation and the appeal in her face. 'Please, Mr Arden,' she breathed.

He nodded in answer, held back one screen end for her and closed it behind him. They separated to wash their hands at the sinks on either side of the small wards. The hall passage doorway was still unscreened and the returned lights were enough to expose the chaos on the ward floor, the paper-chains either trailing down walls from single points, or lying in little heaps, or blown into confetti, and the men that could sit themselves sitting up, lighting cigarettes, and those that were still flat on their backs and beyond reach of their lockers, catching the packets of cigarettes and boxes of matches lobbed by their more mobile neighbours. Only Sam Eccles was not trying to smoke as he was still on his face.

Joe said, 'I'll give you a hand turning Sam, then push off.'

'Thank you, Mr Arden,' said Rose and whilst they turned and sat up Sam, Jill Ashley-Ellis and Midget in dressing-gown and pyjamas and on one armpit crutch, together steered the tea-laden heavy wooden food trolley into the hall. When Joe left MO 1 a few minutes later, the silent West End was sipping hot strong sweet tea, the trolley was in the still silent East End and Jill was handing out the steaming mugs; Rose had righted the desk and vanished to the housemaid's cupboard for a broom, floor-mop, dustpan and brush and two buckets; and the night mechanic from Repairs and Works had arrived with a massive reel of cable and emergency telephone set.

Hospital routine, thought Joe Arden, going out into the cold damp night. There was no wind, not even a breeze, and the air was heavy with smoke and dust and the acrid smell of explosives. The clouds hovering over the new craters hid the shadowy Regency outline of Main Block and its outstretched Nissen hut arms and the figures of the rescue squad ringing the craters with warning flags and ropes and converted their lighted torches to moving flickers of pale, blurred light. The smoke muffled their voices, but not their coughs, or the distant faint hissing of the firemen's hoses dousing the fire the burning aircraft had started in the wood on the far side of the hill. But as he walked quickly towards the huts of the OU, he was oblivious to the cold, the smoke, the coughs, the hoses, the ugly smell of the air, and the new pain in the old wound in his left foot.

His body was between the wards. His head and heart were in MO 1 as they had been for a period he could time to the second.

When he had flung himself face down on the ground floor corridor of Main Block a few yards from the staff entrance at the back of the building, he had instinctively glanced at his watch before closing his eyes against the explosion of the first bomb. Whilst all hell had been let loose, he'd been in his own hell and that was a hell that had distant and modern roots, and reeked of the sickly-sour smell of fresh-spilled blood, and was filled with flying objects that were unrecognisable as parts of human bodies, and was deafened by the dreadful barrage of noise. The memory of the distant hell that he had known for a few months before his eighteenth birthday, had haunted his sleep until he was nearly 30. And if, in comparison, tonight's hell had been momentary, it had been long enough to him to see in imagination what he might see in reality when he reached what remained of MO 1. And being no longer a boy, frightened for his own and his friends' lives, but a mature man desperately concerned for the wounded men in his care and in agony for the girl he loved, in tonight's hell he had hit the bottom of the pit.

Hospital routine, he thought, nothing changes it; the dead must wait upon the living; the living must wait upon the living; and living, itself, must wait upon time – unless time runs out first. 'Everything's in other hands . . . time alone is ours' so said Seneca, he thought, and grimaced with a bitterness that transformed his face to that of another man. Not if one was an Englishman living in the civilised twentieth century. Not if one was no more than a boy and in love with a girl for the first time and longed for life, and love, and hope – and a left leg and two feet.

His tongue could be quick; his anger had always been slow to rouse but once roused burned with a white and terrible heat. He shivered with rage on the doorstep of Hut 9 and had to put his hands in his pockets and clench his fists to control himself before he could unlatch the door.

It opened into a smallish, wide wooden-walled corridor beyond which lay the long, 40-bed ward. All the ward lights were on; all the decorations and the Christmas tree were intact; and the twenty-five bedpatients, all soldiers unable to get home for Christmas leave, were drinking mugs of hot, strong, sweet tea, and laughing and talking amongst themselves and to their two night nurses, with the mild euphoria of those, that with their immediate companions – whether friends or strangers – have just survived an air raid unharmed.

They welcomed him, warmly. 'So Jerry's fetched you up early, too, sir. Noisy basket, Jerry – if you'll pardon my French, nurses – but from what the nurses and young Mr Lomax been saying, looks like he needs to get in a bit of time on target practice, Jerry does. Not got the one hit on the one ward, he didn't, and not even knocked our stockings down off our beds, but our night nurses say if we touches 'em before morning proper, they'll have all Hut 9 on a charge! Not too early to wish you a happy Christmas, is it, sir? And if you'll not mind my asking, sir, come down the chimney, did you? That where you picked up that bit of dust?'

Joe smiled pleasantly – and knew how he managed it. Experience, he thought. Bloody experience. 'Chimney was a bit messy, sergeant, but thanks very much and a very happy Christmas to you all. I'm glad to see you're enjoying a cuppa.'

'Buckshee, sir. Got to thank Jerry for that.' The sergeant had both legs in traction and his left arm in plaster. He raised the mug in his good right hand. 'Ta, Jerry,' he beamed. 'Stop by, anytime.'

Joe went on smiling and chatting to them pleasantly and as his hands were back in his duffle coat pockets, no one in Hut 9 saw his fists were so clenched that his knuckles were white.

Part III

February, 1944.

10

They stopped on the edge of the pavement in Whitehall to use the Belisha crossing that had an island and was just beyond the Home Office on the opposite side.

'Hold it, Mrs Weston' Joe caught her elbow lightly then dropped his hand as if the contact with the fine black broadcloth of her jacket had given him an acute electric shock before the oncoming red double-decker bus went by. The bus windows were newly crisscrossed with anti-blast strips covering the dirty, peeling, old strips, and the youngish clippie wore the straps of her leather money satchel, ticket and ticket-clipping machine over one shoulder and the buckled chinstraps of an old, black painted tin hat over the other.

He glanced at the crowded bus. 'Recalling your comment at lunch that Jerry's return bout is half emptying London, I must say that if I believe you, thousands wouldn't. Place looks as crowded as when I was last up in November. Right. Over – no, not quite.' They had to wait on the island and as they waited their heads swung in unison towards the heavily sandbagged Cenotaph.

Rose looked from the guarded monument to his guarded face. Earlier this morning he'd attended an ex-patient's Medical Board in Millbank and he had on his best professional suit. She had never before seen him in daylight in that suit, and she remembered seeing him in it for the first time on one early morning in MO 1 that now seemed – and was – lifetimes back. She had thought he looked good in it then; more than good, she thought now. In the early afternoon sunshine that hinted of spring, his well-groomed, slightly curly light brown hair looked fairer and had no traces of grey, and his strong face that was tanned by constant exposure to the country weather between the wards of Everly Place, looked so much younger that it was hard to believe he had fought, if only for a few months, in 'the war to end war'. Fought and survived, she thought, if not well enough to fight again, well enough to reach his prime in another world war and to learn from that most painful and undeniable of all lessons, personal experience, the hideous futility of false hopes and false slogans. Only twenty years of uneasy peace. Only just enough time for another generation to be old enough to wear uniforms and tote guns – but not old enough to vote. I'm twenty-five, she thought, and I still haven't been able to vote. Stephen just made it. Not Johnny. She looked quickly away towards Parliament Square. She didn't see it.

Joe was so conscious of her every movement that he glanced down involuntarily at her half-averted face beneath a small, dark mink pillbox tilted over her white forehead almost to brush her right black eyebrow. The hat matched her above-elbow cape that had an upstanding collar and both had been her nineteenth birthday present from her grandfather and, like the black coat and skirt she'd bought in Paris in early 1939, until today unused for four years. The texture of the fur gave her creamy complexion a pearly glow, and the exquisite cut of her suit enhanced the smallness of her waist. The combination made her look so devastatingly attractive and unselfconsciously elegant – as the really elegant invariably are – that each time he looked at her his head renewed its long struggle with his suddenly speeding heart.

She felt his glance and in self-defence asked primly, 'Jerry filling FO 1 and the huts from here, Mr Arden?'

'More than adequately.'

'How about Anzio?'

'One convoy to date. Another's due later this week from the gen I picked up this morning. I also gathered – though reading between the lines in the papers and BBC news it's

176

been obvious – this show at Cassino's being arguably the bloodiest since we landed in Italy. Right.' He didn't touch her again. 'Over we go.'

It was late February, and their first meeting since Rose's set had returned to London on the 29th of December after working the previous night. They had had to move immediately out of the Night Home to allow their replacements to be in bed by 3.0 that afternoon, but once in London they had been given three instead of the two nights off due after their two extra weeks on nights. In the second week of January they had taken Hospital Finals and one week later, on the 21st, the German long-range bombers had returned to attacking England in force, with London their main target. Two days later, on 23rd, the Allies had landed at Anzio and met such fierce resistance that the landing had taken six days; on the 4th of February, the Allied offensive at Cassino had begun; last week, on the 15th, Monte Cassino had been destroyed by Allied bombs, but that battle was still raging and London was still being blitzed.

Once more all over London there were new mounds of rubble and craters amongst those still waiting their turn to be filled in or flattened from the major blitzes of '40 and '41; new gaps and jagged outlines in the old, gaping, jagged skylines; newly damaged tenement, council, Edwardian, Victorian, Georgian, Regency and mock-Tudor 1930s houses like old dolls' houses with the fronts torn off. And on the exposed upper floors the unsalvage-able furniture was caked with dust, plaster, lime, and the grime of centuries. On the filthy, cracked walls the filthy glassless or cracked mirrors, pictures, and framed photo-graphs hung askew. All the occupants of those houses had moved elsewhere; either to neighbours, or relatives, or friends, or out of London, or to hospitals, or graves.

They walked on to Parliament Square and then to St James's Park, in a silence that was permeated by their mutual, secret conviction that their ability to take an after-lunch stroll together when both were temporarily free of professional and totally of personal ties, was little short of a miracle. For the last week since Joe had written his first letter to Rose asking her to lunch with him today and she had accepted by return, they had been as secretly haunted by the thought that the war would prevent this meeting. Rose's mind had contained the fear in that thought with the words – either he or I won't be able to get away from the hospital. Joe's had restrained it to the 'not improbable' that had been all he had allowed himself in this context from the third week in January.

This morning in the train up, he had worked out, almost academically, that if he left his terminus, Waterloo, by the side exit into York Road, he would see more swiftly if what remained of Martha's had had a direct hit last night. And then a ticket-collector had given him immediate, overwhelming, if temporary relief. 'Another nice day, sir, and another nice night. Copped it down Lewisham and New Cross way, mind. Fair's fair. Turn and turn about.'

Whose turn tonight? Today? Tomorrow? Joe frowned briefly at his thoughts as he walked on knowing that, but for Jerry, he wouldn't be risking seeing her again and that all his self-rationalisations about wanting to be sure she had recovered from her grief and shock at Johnny's death, though true, were still rationalisations. He loved her too much, he wanted and needed to see her too much, to have been able to ignore this opportunity of doing so – when it was not improbable that he might not have another – and this was also the first chance he'd had to get to London since she had left Everly Place without either he, or MO 1 in person being able to wish her so much as 'all the best.'

On the morning of Rose's last night on duty the new orthopaedic registrar had finally arrived and during that night another convoy had come in. It had been Mr Hodges's night on call, but as the registrar was new, Joe's offer to come back and help admit the convoy had been gratefully accepted by his older colleague. They had sent fourteen grossly wounded stretcher-cases to MO 1. Once Casualty had eventually been cleared, medical ethics, hospital etiquette, and above both, Joe's powers of imagination and self-control had prevented him from looking in on MO 1 before he left the hospital. And as he had walked wearily, with his slight limp more pronounced than usual, past the dark long low outline of the villa that had new glass in its broken windows, newly dried paint replacing the padding on the rear walls of SWs 3 and 4, and new faces in all its formerly empty beds, for the sake only of Rose's bruised heart he had been relieved that this last night would leave her no spare second for personal reflections. He had been certain that if it later occurred to her that he hadn't stopped in to say 'cheers', she would understand his professional motives for this.

His judgement here had been right. All that night Rose had been too busy to remember it was probably her last chance of seeing him and in the morning she kept Ellie, and then for the first time Sister MO 1, waiting. But even Ellie, when unable to start sweeping the ward before 7.40, had remarked that she, for one, knew there was a war on, and Sister MO 1, that as exceptional circumstances demanded exceptional attitudes she was prepared to overlook her night senior's inability to complete her written report before 8.15. After the verbal report, 'Thank you, Nurse Weston. Good luck in your Hospital Finals. Off you go, quickly. Good morning.'

It had been raining hard and Jill Ashley-Ellis had been too exhausted to remember it was Rose's last night and already gone home. Rose had ridden alone down to the main entrance and then jumped off her bicycle to look back at MO 1 through the grey curtain of rain and the faces in her mind.

Two were uppermost.

Joe's face, professionally pleasant, rising from the desk. 'I'll see myself off, nurse. The registrar'll be on this job tomorrow night but as I'll probably still be in the hospital when you come on I expect I'll see you again before you leave us. We'll miss you,' he added pleasantly and had gone before she could answer. And Johnny's face in the spinal carriage with the old service cap that looked too big for him tilted forward to a guardsman's angle. 'When you gotta go, you gotta go.'

She had turned away, scooted to mount, and as she rode on alone down the empty, muddy, winding lane she had brushed upwards the brim of her navy outdoor uniform hat to let the rain wash the tears from her exhausted face.

St James's Park was emptier than would have been usual at that hour on such a fine day. There were few passers-by when they stopped on the wooden bridge over the lake, on the side that faced Duck Island, Horse Guards Parade, and the backs of Whitehall. Through the bare trees that on that side fringed the Park, the sandbagged, concrete pillbox-shaped structures that dotted the parade ground were soft-ened by the sunshine into natural growths rather than man-made items; and over the width of the greater London sky, the fleet of poised, great grey barrage balloons that trailed long grey cables, was silvered by the sun. The water on the lake sparkled and rippled peacefully under the bridge, and a little posse of dripping ducks clustered round the feet of an elderly woman feeding them crumbs from an old brown paper bag as she sat on the wooden bench that backed the lakeside path. The bench was backed by the grass that had the first gentle film of young green.

Joe glanced at the sky and mentally measured their immediate distances from the nearest entrance to the public air-raid shelter under Parliament Square and to West-minster and St James's Park Tube stations. He had not used one public shelter since the war started, but being a Londoner, in common with his fellows, regarded the Tubes as his personal shelters, and on his own only took cover when he heard aircraft, ack-ack fire or both. But as Rose was with him, he was determined to rush her to the nearest shelter at the first wail of an alert.

'I've not yet congratulated you on passing Hospital Finals.'

She looked at him quickly. 'Thanks. How did you know?'

'Sister MO 1.' He paused, then prompted, 'Didn't you do rather well?'

She enchanted him by blushing. 'Quite.'

His eyes smiled. 'Let's have it, Mrs Weston. Sister said you got a medal. What make?'

'Only a Bronze.'

He said deadpan, 'Even Homer sometimes nods.'

She laughed with him and at herself, 'I asked for that. How is Sister?'

'As ever, the rock upon which her ward stands.' He paused again, then added in a different tone, 'Sam's being another.'

They looked at each other in an accord that was new in this meeting but dated from the dawning of that particular understanding that is the beginning of love, that had been born in both on the night of the first incoming Salerno wounded.

Rose said, 'Sam began being that on Christmas morning. Did you know he took over the MO 1 book on Christmas night?' He nodded. 'You were right. All he needed was for someone to re-light the spark. Your piano struck the match, but Johnny set it blazing when he died singing.'

'The piano was your idea, but you're more right than you can know about Johnny. No line this, but a fact. Johnny's spirit is living on in Sam. He's a different man and running MO 1 as Johnny did and got his eye on the chap that'll take over when he's transferred. That'll be shortly. The back's healed well, he's in a chair all day and keeping him in it is getting problematical as he keeps trying to stand. He's determined to make it unaided.'

Her eyes mirrored her sadness for Johnny and relief for Sam. 'That's wonderful, but – can he, ever? Isn't that impossible?'

He marvelled at the sweet expressiveness of her face and his own blindness when he had mistaken her for a primly unimaginative little Dutch doll. 'How many times have you seen patients prove all the bloody books and specialists wrong? Lost count?' He read the answer in her eyes. 'So've I, over and over, having been qualified seventeen years.'

'So you have,' she said vaguely, as her mind shot off at a tangent to her immediate reaction to his letter. Had he been a registrar or houseman she would have taken it as a much desired if totally unexpected, opening gambit; coming from a senior member of the Staff it had nearly given her a coronary from joy, and left her deeply confused. Her Victorian grandmother would have regarded it as a straight declaration of intentions, but she had never known Joe Arden. As Rose did, she had managed to persuade her present ward sister – who objected on principle to changing her off duty rota – to change her this week's day off from yesterday to today, by announcing politely but firmly that if necessary she would take her request to Matron as she had to be free today to attend to urgent, personal matters.

She turned from the thought and Joe's watching eyes and looking down at the water, she thought aloud. 'Johnny would've been so bucked for Sam. "Big-Hearted Johnny, that's me." He was. Period.'

He looked down at her in passionate concern. 'He was. You must still miss him.'

'I always do. For ages.'

'Always?'

She looked at him and said simply, 'When I've loved a patient. We aren't meant to love them but sometimes I can't help it. I've loved others – men – women – kids – and when they've died – and so many did – something of me seemed to die with them. It's like a bit of my heart dropping off. The bit that died with Johnny was the biggest and the most agony as he was – Johnny.'

'I know.'

Again their eyes had met and mentally they were so close that they could have been holding each other with both hands, though his were in his trouser pockets and hers on the wooden rail. She said, 'I thought you did,' and he inclined his head.

For a minute or so they stood in silence and as still as they had at Johnny's bedside after they covered his cold, boyish dead face. Then they walked slowly off the bridge and along the lakeside path talking of Midget, back home in Scotland, Major Chalmers, up in a wheelchair, Major Williams, up on crutches and OC kitchen crew, the

182

Brigadier, due off traction next week, and George Hall due out of his spinal plaster at the end of this one. 'They still miss their Snow White,' he said, smiling.

Her eyes laughed, 'I wasn't supposed to know that. I'd have had to have been deaf not to. I miss them too – I loved MO 1 and Hut 9. I like Rachel, my new ward and I expect I'll love it by the time I have to leave though I mayn't have to.'

His heart seemed to stop in his new anxiety. 'Has your medal earned you a staff nurse's job up here?'

'Well – sort of.'

'I –' he stopped the word 'feared' in time 'thought it would. Civvy hospitals being allowed to hang on longer to their best nurses, as residents. Presumably, from what you've just said, you intend taking it?'

Rose didn't answer at once; and, as she chose her words, she stopped walking and looked up at the sky. And stopping beside her, he saw beneath the delicate, youthful oval curve of her face, the strength that had once astonished Sue Kirby and would once have done the same to him, but now that he knew her, had a very different effect. If MO 1 could see her now, he thought, they'd say, 'Snow White's going into action.' He put his hands back in his pockets, slightly hunched his shoulders and waited.

Rose turned to him slowly. She had now recognised his fundamental motive for suggesting this date, and even although that insight seemed too wonderful for belief, because it was true, the war that was their enemy had become her ally. Every instinct she possessed insisted that she must use this moment and ignore the attitudes and conventions instilled in her from early childhood. She said, 'I don't know, Mr Arden, as whether I stay on as a civvy nurse until we've won the war, or join the Army in a month or two – a few of my set've already been called-up – doesn't depend on me. Jerry aside –' she gestured dismissively, 'what I'm going to do, depends on you. If you'll marry me I'll stay in England, if you won't, I'll go overseas.'

His face tightened as if she had hit him, physically, and for several seconds he just looked at her in a silence that for both was deafened by the drumming of their respective temporal pulses. 'You – want to marry me?' He queried quietly, politely.

She blushed, but neither her eyes nor voice wavered. 'Yes, please. Only –' she hesitated then spat out the words as bitterly as once to Johnny 'my nickname at school was Trigger. Trig, to my chums.'

His set, watchful face had concealed from habit rather than intention, the sudden confusion of his own instincts and near-overwhelming sensation of astounded, joy. But her bitterness hurt him for her, and he flushed deeply, and breathed as if he had been running, though he spoke almost lightly, 'Hell of a lot better than Spit, Spitty, or Big Bertha, and if not as apt as Snow White, it probably was when you were a skinny little kid in pigtails. You didn't pick up your ability to move like quicksilver or the speed with which you can slip the safety-catch, overnight.' The glance he gave her shining black bun was an open caress. 'Did you wear that in pigails?'

The sudden upsurge of hope nearly throttled her. 'Yes,' was all she could manage.

'So I've imagined.' He looked into her face and she saw the passionate love, tenderness, wonder, and the anxiety – the agonised anxiety – in his eyes. He said, in a voice he had never used to her before, 'You must – you obviously do – know that I love you very – very much and that there's nothing I want more than to marry you, but more than "Trigger's" in the way. I'm forty-two. You're only twenty-five and so – so enchantingly young.'

She hit back, at once. 'After your war, how young were you at twenty-five, Mr Arden?' The formality slipped out from habit and raised the same fleeting smile in their eyes. 'Twenty-five on the outside only, I'll bet. Like me.' She tapped her cape. 'Like Johnny was – like Midget is – like all the others in all the troops' wards that are still boys on paper. And I'd a head start. I'd stopped being young before I started nursing.'

He looked her over as she stood looking up at him and looking so young, and decorative that to the casual observer it must seem that she could never have heard of work, of pain, of grief. And, momentarily, he saw in his mind her face in his torchlight when she emerged from the screens round Johnny's body.

He took a long breath. 'I'll accept that nothing beats a war for pitching youth into premature maturity. For all that, seventeen years is one hell of a difference. When I'm pushing sixty, you'll just be my present age.'

She looked deliberately up and around the sky. 'Would you bet on either of those?'

'Stop that, Rose!' The stern retort was cracked with pain. 'There's no need for you to hit under the belt with Jerry on the job.' He looked around. 'We've got to talk. We can't do that here. Too bloody exposed in every sense. What time do you have to get back to Martha's?'

'Not till eleven.'

'Good. I can see you back in good time before I get the last train down at ten-forty. Bill Hodges is on tonight, but I must get back in case anything odd crops up. And I must –' he added with a tremor in his deep voice 'get us away from this damned public place before I lose what's left of my sanity and provide an item for tomorrow's papers that'll give MO 1 a field-day, but not our respective hospitals.' He took another look around at the near-empty park. 'No cameras in sight, but with you looking like an exquisite fashion plate and I –' he touched his jacket 'as if I've just escaped from the nearest Ministry, a snap of you in my arms could be worth a few bob, and very possibly more if the news editor has a good memory for faces. And no man –' he paused, 'no man, could forget yours, Rose. As for how you look today –' again he paused, 'daren't comment in public. But – er – thank you.'

Again, she blushed. 'Thank you.'

'A great pleasure.' They smiled at each other. 'Right. Let's find some spot that's relatively private and underground so that we don't have to shift if Jerry starts playing up. One of the hotels on the river or up west?'

'River, please, even though we won't be able to see it.' Her eyes were alight with love, happiness and laughter.

185

'What I love about the river is that the buildings on its banks have to have lovely strong deep basements.'

'Quite. What's more, nearer.' He drew her arm through his and enclosed her small hand in his and she felt the sudden tension of his arm muscles and the gentle clasp of his strong hand, and she knew that she had won this private war.

They walked as sedately out of St James's Park as they had walked in, and again they walked in silence. But this time they walked close together in a silence that was alive with hope and harboured no unshared secret places and neither once looked up at the armada of great grey barrage balloons that trailed long, lethal, cables and hovered over their heads.

THE END

A WEEKEND IN THE GARDEN
by Lucilla Andrews
The second novel of the trilogy begun with
ONE NIGHT IN LONDON

June 1951 . . . it was a hot, hectic weekend for the staff of
The Garden, the small cottage hospital in Kent, where anti-
biotics were regarded as the new wonderdrugs and the
patients' wireless headphones a luxury . . .

Catherine Jason had become a theatre sister at The Garden
to be near her sick husband, Mark, a patient at the TB clinic
nearby. Also working at The Garden, as a locum, was Dr
George Macdonald, an old colleague of the Jason's who has
fallen deeply in love with Catherine . . .

As the weekend passed Catherine and George realised that
for them, nothing would ever be the same again . . .

'Compulsive reading . . . is a vivid reminder of life in the
immediate post-war years and of the conditions in which
nurses worked'
Nursing Times

0 552 11909 1   95p

THE PRINT PETTICOAT
by Lucilla Andrews

In the country Maternity Unit of a London teaching hospital, Joanna Anthony enjoyed both her job as nursery staff nurse, and her love for the man who had been her 'steady' for five years. Two other young men, one an old friend, the other a new one, watched and shared her hectically busy professional life.

When she moved back to London to share a flat with her great friend Beth (and wallow in the luxury of 'living out of hospital' for the first time) Allan and Marcus were regular 'droppers in'. And then a serious illness took her back to her parent hospital as a patient, and in a hospital bed she finally faced reality – and happiness . . .

0 552 11385 9   75p

IN AN EDINBURGH DRAWING ROOM
by Lucilla Andrews
The third novel of the trilogy begun with
ONE NIGHT IN LONDON.

There were three of them on the London to Edinburgh
Express. Jason, the young, overworked Senior Accident
Officer at St. Martha's, son of a St. Martha's medical
family, returning to his family for Hogmanay.

Francesca Turner, nurse at Murrayfield General, lovely,
lonely, fighting bad dreams . . . And Dave Oliver, clever,
ill, and still not over his divorce.

The three of them, not knowing each other, not caring –
until the train leapt the vandalised track and the journey
became a nightmare.

Then Jason, Francesca, and Dave – and Mary, the young
nurse who was to care for them – found their lives physically
and emotionally intertwined.

0 552 12439 7   £1.50

MANGO WALK
by Rhona Martin

It began in the Blitz . . .

He was a seaman, returning on shore leave to find his home a mound of rubble and his family destroyed.

She was a tiny waif, bereft and as destitute as he. He called her Honey.

To begin with they just needed each other – because they had no one else, and then, as Honey grew, and as the years changed him, the tenderness, the caring became a deep and abiding love, stronger than the conflicts that threatened them, more passionate than the controls others tried to enforce.

'*Mango Walk* is only too convincing. It has narrative power, sentimentality and compassion'
Martyn Goff, *Daily Telegraph*

0 552 11872 9   £1.75

A SCATTERING OF DAISIES
by Susan Sallis

Will Rising had dragged himself from humble beginnings to his own small tailoring business in Gloucester – and on the way he'd fallen violently in love with Florence, refined, delicate, and wanting something better for her children.

March was the eldest girl, the least loved, the plain, unattractive one who, as the family grew, became more and more the household drudge. But March, a strange, intelligent, unhappy child, had inherited some of her mother's dreams. March Rising was determined to break out of the round of poverty and hard work, to find wealth, and love, and happiness.

0 552 12375 7   £1.95

A SELECTED LIST OF TITLES AVAILABLE
FROM CORGI BOOKS

While every effort is made to keep prices low, it is sometimes necessary to increase prices at short notice. Corgi Books reserve the right to show new retail prices on covers which may differ from those previously advertised in the text or elsewhere.

The prices shown below were correct at the time of going to press.

ORDER FORM

All these books are available at your book shop or newsagent, or can be ordered direct from the publisher. Just tick the titles you want and fill in the form below.

CORGI BOOKS, Cash Sales Department, P.O. Box 11, Falmouth, Cornwall.

Please send cheque or postal order, no currency.

Please allow cost of book(s) plus the following for postage and packing:

U.K. Customers—Allow 55p for the first book, 22p for the second book and 14p for each additional book ordered, to a maximum charge of £1.75.

B.F.P.O. and Eire—Allow 55p for the first book, 22p for the second book plus 14p per copy for the next seven books, thereafter 8p per book.

Overseas Customers—Allow £1.00 for the first book and 25p per copy for each additional book.

NAME(Block Letters)...

ADDRESS..

....